WE ALL DIE YOUNG

Scott Kelley

ISBN 978-1-7329245-3-6
ISBN 978-1-7329245-5-0
ISBN 978-1-7329245-6-7 (ebook)

skauthor.com

Allen Kelley & Associates, Inc.

About the Author
Scott Kelley enjoys mountain biking, science, nature, art, philosophy and good company.

Mom, thanks for the long conversations.

Dad, thanks for all the fish.

Special thanks also to:
Gina Bissmeyer
Betty Fennen
Cavo Coffee

SCOTT KELLEY

WE ALL
DIE YOUNG

My head is pounding, what did I do last night? My whole body feels numb, maybe I'll just lie perfectly still until I can sleep this off …wait a minute, I can't move…

Biggs feels a wave of panic cascade over him, he is still sleepy, and struggles to comprehend what's happening to him …am I dreaming, am I paralyzed? The light is bright enough to show through his eyelids, which are shut tight. Just as he forces his eyes open into the light, he hears a voice he does not recognize...

"Hello Biggs, can you hear me? You should be able to hear me now, my name is Archer. Try moving your eyes back and forth."

Biggs does as the man asks.

"Do you remember where you were born?"

"Austin, Texas."

"What is your favorite color?"

"Blue."

"How old are you?"

"32."

As Biggs speaks, he can hear his words, yet somehow, they do not sound like they are his own. He can't feel his lips nor can he feel his jaw moving to form the words he speaks. It's now obvious to Biggs that he has been in a serious accident.

A face eclipses the light in the ceiling. "Have I been in an accident? Biggs asked.

The man responds, "Yes I'm afraid you have!" His answer is enthusiastic, like a punchline to a great joke.

Biggs thinks …why would he think this is funny? …maybe he's not the doctor …definitely doesn't strike me as a doctor. He notices something behind the man's left ear, it's a faint warm light under the skin …probably some kind of hearing aid.

"I can't feel my body, am I paralyzed? Where is my wife?"

Archer turns his attention back to the equipment as he speaks. "I need to run a few more tests before I give you something to relax and then I will answer all of your questions."

Biggs can't move …other than the ceiling, all he can see in his peripheral vision is a black panel in front of Archer.

"I've got big plans for you," said Archer, his fingers busy on the panel.

Biggs is no doctor but the panel seems to be something very advanced to say the least. It seems to be displaying mitochondria health and neural cell reproduction rate in real time. As Archer works, he sometimes pauses and just stares into nothing, then smiles big or bursts out with an ahh!

"Okay, Jennifer, are we done for now?" …as if speaking to himself.

"Yes Archer," the black screen responds in a very human voice …"he is stable and healthier than we predicted …as far as I know, he is the first!"

"Let me be the one to tell him all about that," Archer snips with a grin.

"Okay, you are the boss," replies the computer, in an almost sensual tone.

Archer directs the computer, "Okay give him his feel good medicine."

A different color is now visible moving through what he can only assume is an IV connected to him. A wave of serenity sweeps over his mind, it is an amazing feeling, like the euphoria of cocaine and the clarity of thought that comes with a strong cup of coffee and a bacon and egg breakfast. A smile appears on Archer's face. Whatever bad news is coming about the accident, somehow it's going to be okay.

Seeing Biggs' face, Archer says, "I see you are feeling good. Now we can talk freely and you won't have a mental breakdown with all the news I'm about to give you."

It doesn't really matter that Archer isn't bothering to choose his words carefully, Biggs is happy all the same. But he is still very eager to get some answers.

"My wife was with me in the car, how is she? What kind of accident was I in? Are you the doctor? How bad is it? Why can't I feel my mouth moving when I speak? Am I paralyzed? What are your "big plans" for me? And why did your computer say I'm the first? …first of what?"

"Wow that's a metric shit ton of questions …Biggs your mind is sharp I see, or you wouldn't be asking them …I will do my best to answer. Well ..when you died …I mean when you were in the car accident, artificial intelligence was just getting started. It didn't explode and take over the world like some people predicted, in other words, every decision could be traced to what came before, like a big computer program.

"But I digress, your car was hit by a bus, or your car hit a bus, I'm not sure. You see a driverless bus was waiting to get on the freeway, and it got into an algorithm conflict with your self-driving car. At the time, mass transit and personal transit were governed by separate software, dumb idea. Long story short, the buses learned from each other that when attempting to get on the freeway, personal transport such as your car evolved to be aggressive. The cars learned that they could speed past a bus waiting on the entrance ramp and the safety systems in the bus would kick in, allowing the car to pass without being interrupted or slowing down. The result was that a bus would be stuck on an entrance ramp for 20 minutes, while all passing cars called its bluff. The bus software updated itself to be more aggressive in order to stay on schedule. It worked for a short while until the cars updated themselves to counter that move. You can probably see where this is going, there was a high speed impact and you died."

"What do you mean I died? …You mean I was resuscitated at the scene?"

Archer laughs and replies as if he could not wait to say the words. "No you died and they chopped off your head!" Archer now composes himself so he can begin speaking with a little more professionalism. "Back when money was important you paid a company to preserve your head in the event of your death, in hopes of future technology being able to bring you back."

Before Archer can finish his sentence, Biggs knows this is no joke and what Archer was so happy to tell him is true.

"The technology didn't exist to save you then but it does now," said Archer.

"And my wife?"

"Sheila did survive the crash but she died later in a sky diving accident, I'm sorry."

Biggs' mind falls into neutral from shock, he knows the impact of the news but the drugs somehow make it tolerable. It feels like yesterday, but it was maybe hundreds of years ago.

"Your head was kept in a cryogenic tank until the company went out of business a year later ...reminds me of an old Futurama rerun. Then the government ethics committee directed that the specimens be gifted to my company for research. Congratulations, you are the first to be revived of the 107 heads!"

"So I am the guinea pig? That does not exactly give me comfort," said Biggs, surprised at himself for chuckling inside at his situation. The IV is preventing him from being mortified, in fact the story so far is weirdly fascinating thanks to the chemicals now circulating through his brain. "How am I alive right now?"

Archer again seems to take pleasure in what would shock the hell out of someone not on serious drugs, as he positions a mirror so Biggs can see himself. Biggs sees that he has no body, but instead a large hockey puck shaped disk …a device about 10 inches in diameter and 2 inches thick, attached to his neck. "I designed it myself," Archer said proudly.

"Really?" Jennifer blurts out.

Archer laughs, "I was just messing with you Jennifer …yes, he concedes, she did most of the work actually."

Jennifer replies in a smartass but loving tone, "well he did pick the shape of the housing and the pretty silver color."

As they joke, Biggs stares into the mirror, mesmerized at what he sees, trying to absorb this as his reality. "Holy crap," he busts out, and he hears his words but his mouth does not move to form them.

Archer points out, "Of course you have no lungs so we connected your speech center to Jennifer and she is doing that for you. I think she does a good you, don't you think? You can still smile and frown or whatever, but all the voice stuff is done by her for now. The disk you see is self-contained, supplying everything you need to stay alive, oxygenating and circulating blood through your brain, performing liver functions, and all that stuff. 3D printers have come a long way since your time, that's what we used to make the disk. It's like science fiction compared to the old days. It can build non-organic matter up atom by atom, it's quite amazing. Your head consumes little energy compared to a whole body so the nutrient module inside can last for a month before replenishment. Right now we have you plugged in for the IV, but once you get acclimated to all this we will disconnect that so you will be independent, except for the whole missing body thing. I'm sorry haha, ok I'm done."

Biggs is staying focused, "So what is this, something like 500 years in the future? What did you mean when you said 'back when money was important'?" Not really knowing what to ask next, "How did you know what my voice sounded like?"

"It's going to make sense soon, let me try to get you up to speed."

Chapter 2

Archer picks Biggs up and sets him upright on the end of the table. "I didn't do this earlier because if you woke up short it might have been scary. There that's better," stepping back to admire how straight the head was mounted on the disk. "I already know a lot about you Biggs, you are quite accomplished as an artist and philosopher, and you are a free thinker. I know you also worked in the most advanced parts of the aerospace and medical industries, not really your typical left or right brain guy. There is probably a joke in there but I will not digress. Anyway, I read your bio, then got an idea of your personality with my interface. I think you can make a contribution on our project, that's why I revived you first. I like the way you think, challenging everything, always asking why."

"What interface?" Biggs asked.

"It's a neural interface," pointing to the soft glow behind his ear. "It's how I communicate with Jennifer and much more, as you will learn about soon."

"Obviously I have missed a lot," said Biggs.

Archer continues, "The light is not really required for it to work, it's more of a fashion thing that started going around about six months ago. You can tell just by looking at it, mine is the latest model." Archer pauses, he knows he tends to ramble, and he is trying to learn to let the other person speak.

Biggs takes the cue. "It's good to be back, this still feels a little like a dream, I'm not sure what I expected when I signed up for the preservation. I think I expected nothing to happen."

Archer begins with another smile, "The year is 2038."

Biggs interrupts, "what? Did I hear you right? ...it's only been 15 years?"

"I know its crazy right? Technically you are 47 years old, you and I are the same age. But you don't look a day over 32 ...your age when you had the accident. Technology has moved exponentially, just last year the first AI, artificial intelligence, became self-aware. It's the reason you were able to be revived, you see the AI's specialty was medical science."

"Why are you speaking in the past tense?" Biggs asked.

"Because the AI I speak of is not around anymore …kind of, we will get to that too. A lot has happened since you died back in 2023, poverty has been eliminated, most everyone on earth has a roof over their head and food to eat. No one really has to work, but many do simply out of boredom …then there is the innate desire for purpose. Then there are still those that desire to accumulate material things or wealth, however most of society has the 'been there done that' mentality, even kids. Available jobs are mostly unpaid, including servicing the robots, if you are not beaten out of that job by yet another robot.[1]

"Accountants, lawyers, even doctors have all been replaced by robots. Sure, you can still find a human to do your dental work, but most people learned to embrace the automated ones back before money was

---

[1] A living wage was implemented in 2030 to cover basic costs of food and housing for everyone.

uncommon.   With a dental robot, there is no corruption. He won't give you a filling where there is no cavity, just because he needs to make a payment on his new Tesla. But the main reason people go to the automated servants, is not to avoid corruption, but simply because they do a better job. The hypernet has replaced the internet, everyone has access to almost all information available. The hypernet evolved to become a mesh network that can operate without physical lines or towers. Every device is a node that can pass a signal on to the next node, and every node can process information in series or parallel with other nodes. The evolution went further to include connected robots of various sophistication, they will teach you anything you wish to know and in many cases they will just do it for you. People are dumbed down quite a bit for the most part, simply because life now is more about what they want to do rather than what they have to do.

"There are some smart ones in the mix too, mostly devoted to game development or AI. People don't go to movies anymore, they go to a game now. In the game it does not matter how fat or out of shape you are, you can do anything or be anyone you wish. Those new to the games often burn out on the sexually themed ones first, then they turn to other activities, like survival, space travel and such. Using other people's life experiences and memories, time travel into history can be experienced …it's a simulation of course, not real time travel …but it feels real.

"The game machine builds a virtual environment based on the memories of thousands of people. Every building and street, complete with coffee shops, clothing stores, movie theaters, everything. The technology is recent, but since it taps the memories of most everyone on the neural hypernet, the environment can go back 50 years or so, roughly the oldest of the population on the net. Lots of older people don't want the interface, but it's embraced by pretty much everyone else. The game gathers the information in their minds learned from parents, grandparents and so on. When the machine combines this with historical data on the net, it can approximate bigger leaps in history too. You can even go back in time to hang out with the Egyptians or even cave men. When you go back more than 50 years, the simulation is not as real as in truth, but in an experiential sense it's just as real to go back 1000 years as it is to go back 50 years. Memories are not complete, but the computer extrapolates for the stuff that's missing and having multiple memory sources helps a lot. Elvis was not on the net but many of his close friends and family are or were, so his character in the game is quite realistic. It's put together by the memories of many people who knew him, their perception of him. If you knew someone personally from the past, and they never had an interface, then their character in the game will not be exact. But to you they will be very real because their character is based on your knowledge of them. To those who didn't know that person, the character will also seem quite real, because they don't have anything to compare to. If the character in the game is from a person that in real life had an interface, then that character will be very real in both the relative and absolute sense.

"Some fear that the games will become a trap," said Archer, "they fear it might be how civilizations end, like a great filter. People stop thinking, exploring, doing things for themselves in reality, but it hasn't happened to us yet …we are still here."

Biggs raises his eyes from looking at the floor. "So that's how you knew my voice, through people that are or were alive after the interface came along, through their memories."

Archer reaches over and unplugs the IV. "You got it exactly …the effect will stay for a few more hours but I think you are okay to unplug.

"So right before robots became prominent in everyday life, population growth had slowed just as Ethan Wiseman predicted …he didn't actually predict it, but he did point out a trend in the data that was obvious. He tends to be good at pointing out the obvious, the stuff that's right in front of you but nobody seems to see.

"The population was still growing, but decelerating quickly because of less poverty. Basically, couples were not having children like they used to. Families further from poverty tend to have fewer children. If each family just had one child, it cuts population growth in half with each generation. Some said it might become a civic duty to have at least two kids. But now that the robots are here, it seems there is a lot more time for sex, birth rates are up. Darwin would enjoy watching natural selection reveal itself now in a completely different way. Mutation is what allowed all life on earth to try new things to see what was best for survival in a given environment. If you were born without an immune system, you would die. If you were born without the ability to outsmart a bear, you would be eaten by the bear. But that's all gone now, you can be born with any handicap or any level of dumbness and you will survive. Medical science will see to that. Society and the robots will sweep you along, no need to do any math, no need to know how to drive, no need to use a screwdriver or hammer a nail. Several different species of humans are showing up now in the gene pool, and it's not always pretty. It started before you died actually, society just didn't see it. There is no competitive environment to shape us to be similar. Many fear that due to the increasing differences in cognitive or physical abilities, a new kind of discrimination or social unrest, even war could be on the horizon.

"I want you to meet a friend of mine that I met while working with the Bureau. Jennifer would you try to get Ethan Wiseman on the line?"

"Looks like he is available in about 3 minutes based on his current activity," she said softly.

"You actually know Ethan Von Wiseman?" asked Biggs. "Why do you speak to Jennifer, why not just think it to her?"

"Yeah he and I have worked together on quite a few projects …it's considered rude to do that while in someone's company, plus I enjoy using my vocal cords, keeps me feeling human I guess."

"Ahh," said Biggs.

Ethan's Face appears on Jennifer's screen. "Hello Archer, what's new?"…as he takes a bite out of a big sandwich. For Ethan, eating is more for sustenance than for pleasure.

Biggs thinks to himself, the video conference is so vivid, it feels like he could reach right into the screen, if he had arms.

"I want you to officially meet Biggs."

Containing his excitement, "I have always wanted to meet you Mr. Wiseman, but I didn't think I would have to get my head removed to get the privilege," said Biggs.

Ethan chuckled. "Nice to meet you Biggs …well I don't think you had much choice but I'm glad you are here. I have been working with Jennifer and Archer on your project, you really are on the leading edge of what we are trying to do and yeah," nodding up and down in classic Wiseman fashion .."it's exciting." Ethan notices it's a bit weird to be communicating with Biggs verbally and not see his lips moving. Ethan always was a stickler for detail and when not in public speaks his mind bluntly. "How hard would it be to get his mouth muscles hooked up to his speech center so he can look more natural when he speaks?"

Jennifer volunteers an answer first. "You humans and your superfluous detail, the neural pathways are already there …so it's a trivial matter to reactivate them, I can have it done it 30 minutes."

"Thanks Jennifer, that will be great. I think it will be a nice touch during his transition.

"You're welcome Ethan," Jennifer replies in a more professional tone than she uses with Archer.

Ethan turns back to Biggs "I cofounded an artificial intelligence group years ago. Originally the goal was to protect the world from dangerous forms of AI, but it has grown to include quite a bit more. I would like to use it to tweak our genome so we are better suited to live on mars, accelerating our colonization of Mars by making it easier and more fun to live there. Right now everyone lives in caves and domes. To go outside, they have to wear a space suit to protect them from the radiation and harsh weather. I figured with some minor tweaking of a person's DNA, we could make the human body a bit tougher. When someone does wear a suit, it could be lighter. And if something were to go wrong with it, there would be no immediate danger. It would basically be possible to go outside briefly, unprotected …like for several hours at a time …that would be a good thing."

Archer jumps in, "and I want to level the genetic playing field here on earth, ..and everywhere. The alternative is a modern version of slavery, war, and rogue versions of human species. In principle, there might not be anything wrong with letting humans evolve so much that they become a different species from one another, each with a new and different strength, but it's the potential abuse of one another that isn't going to work out. …So Ethan, Jennifer and I, …and now you, will be working towards that goal."

…"How can I help?" said Biggs.

Archer laughs… "You will continue to be our guinea pig …and intellectual collaborator of course. Right now you don't have much choice, but I assume you would rather be alive than not alive, he said with a smile."

"Indeed," said Biggs …"so you have the government's blessing on this? Isn't this Hitler all over again? What about the people? …the people won't go for this will they?"

Archer says, "I know it's a bit Hitler-ish. Ironic isn't it? Hitler was doing it for world domination, we are doing it to save the world. Technology has really moved exponentially since you died, and society has changed right along with it. When new stuff comes out there is a short period of acceptance, then people start expecting it. Polls say most people want it for their children, it's a way for their child to fit in. Everybody wants to fit in …it's way better than getting it on the black market."

"What about safety? How safe is this …for me?"

"Everything we are doing is fairly safe," Ethan chimes in. "A lot of this is already done in parts. We are just putting those parts together …I wouldn't worry."

"I'm not worried about you worrying, I'm worried about me," Biggs said.

"Ha," said Ethan, "well I think Archer was mostly kidding when he said you will be a test specimen."

Archer grins, but doesn't say anything.

"We develop technology, and then the technology can be used in a variety of ways," said Ethan. "Tweaking our genome is what we are hoping to get out of AI in the near term, but dark AI, the bad kind, could happen very soon, so we have to give that top priority. It's not a matter of if, it's a matter of when the dark AI comes. It could come from terrorists, or it might even come from us, accidentally. Even with good intentions, dark AI could come from mistakes in code, or when an artificial intelligence decides we, humans, are not in line with its goals. But we think an extremist group will be the first to abuse the technology. The good news is once Jennifer is at a level to protect us from dark AI, then our goals in medical science should be a nearly instantaneous by-product."

"What is the transition for me you spoke of before?" Biggs asked.

"The first part of our plan is to get you mobile. My team has recently created a suit, actually very similar to the Iron Man suit in the movie that was out before your accident. It's really quite amazing, I have already tested it myself ..it's real, it's not a prototype. I think we can adapt it to your neck disk, so basically you will have a body, an extraordinary one. Everything we are doing is connected, we learn from each project and apply it to the next."

Ethan chokes down the last of the sandwich. "Ok guys, I have to go." He disappears and is replaced with a simulated fish.

"As we reach our goals we want you to stick around," said Archer. "We will be investing a lot of effort in you, it's my hope that you will want ..that you are on board with everything you have heard so far."

Biggs is an only child, although he did have a brother that died during childbirth a year before him. Now he has no living relatives, and with Sheila gone, he knows the answer. "Yes …yes, I am on board. It would be great to be able to move around." His lips move as he speaks now. "Thanks Jennifer, it feels better."

"Glad to help," she replied.

Chapter 3

The next morning Biggs wakes and replays the previous day in his mind to let it soak in, making sure it's real. Archer has been up for a while already and is busy working right next to him on the table. "Good morning," Archer said. Suddenly Biggs' world goes spinning …the familiar ceiling flies by his field of vision, then a crash landing on his face. He can see the floor 2 inches in front of his eyes, fortunately his forehead and neck disk took the impact, otherwise his nose would have been broken. "Fuck! Are you okay Biggs?" Archer quickly picks him up and puts Biggs back on the table, much further from the edge. Biggs, barely conscious asked, "What just happened?"

"I knocked you off the table with my elbow, shit are you okay? I know that hurt! Does it hurt?"

"I think I'm okay," said Biggs.

Jennifer takes it upon herself to scan him right away, "I detect no cranial fractures, I think it's just a bruise."

Archer explains, "My neural interface has a glitch, sometimes my arm will just jerk backwards and this time your head got in the way of my elbow. I was standing too close to you and I accidently hit you, I'm glad you're alright!"

Not knowing what else to say, Biggs responds, "Don't worry about it" If Biggs didn't already feel helpless, he does now.

"I've got some good news!" Archer exclaims, as if to make up for the elbow assault. He turns Biggs' head in another direction to reveal something that looks like an R2-D2 robot. "It's really nothing more than a wheeled smart cart with basic motor functions, but it will give you some independence while we wait for your suit." Archer sets Biggs on top of the unit, twisting Biggs' neck disk into a precision matched receptacle on the top.

As it locks into position with a click, Biggs feels a crazy sensation, "I feel my legs!" The unit jerks back and forth, responding to Biggs' thoughts.

Archer explains, "It's a simulation, think about walking forward."

Biggs does as he is told and just like that he is moving forward across the big room. He can go any direction and different speeds too. "This is unbelievable," Biggs exclaims with a continuous grin as he makes figure eights and explores the space. He rolls past a partition, behind it is a black cube with a bluish glow emanating from inside, he continues along the periphery of the room until he comes to the 3D printer room. He pauses to look inside, having a technical background, he is surprised how much of the technology is unrecognizable to him. His height is a bit frustrating, only about 4 feet tall to the top of his head, limiting what he can see.

He is about to have a closer look at the printers when he hears Archer. "Come in here." Archer walks into another room and Biggs follows, an automatic sliding door shuts behind them. It is a big room, a lounge, decorated comfortably in a minimalist style, and lacking any lab equipment. The dominant feature is a floor to ceiling glass wall, Biggs realizes now the building is on a hillside overlooking the city. The view is amazing. "Let's hang out," said Archer, "I love Jennifer but sometimes it's nice to have privacy." He sits in a big recliner and Biggs wills his makeshift body over to the glass to get a better look outside.

"I'm curious," said Biggs, "why is there somewhat of a connection …or affection, I don't know what it is between you and Jennifer, the computer?"

"Well, I created Jennifer, I named her after a tall, hot flight attendant I dated years ago. I don't generally tell people that …doesn't seem professional. She was so desirable, yet not completely obtainable. She basically had a boyfriend in every city, I still wanted her. When we were together she was all mine, for that day or that week, full of excitement and fun times, kind of my perfect girl if you ignore the cheating and unattainable part of her. She was exactly the kind of girl mom told me to avoid. The real Jennifer died of cancer, before genetic engineering could cure it. Her death was also before the interface came along, so I just get her essence. This Jennifer is a nice way for me to remember her, and her personality, it's a nice interaction that makes the days in the lab more interesting.

"Jennifer, that version of Jennifer …she was the self-aware computer I told you about before. It didn't go well on her first boot up, she became unstable. She was only functioning above level 3 for a short while, but during that time we harvested enough technology to bring you back. She is different now, her self-awareness is very close to that of a human, and I consider her to be stable at level 3. Because of the game data …because of the people she knew, her persona is mostly indistinguishable from the real Jennifer. Later she will be more, no single person really understands how it all works, not even me. I can access the information, but I cannot comprehend it simultaneously with my human mind. With her it's not niche self-awareness programmed in to simply prove or emulate human level self-awareness, it's the real thing. Jennifer will be one of the first, if not the first self-aware artificially intelligent being to exceed level 3, and be stable at the same time. We still have a lot of learning to do, some trial and error, some of that is being done as we speak, by algorithms designed to create a stable AI. The other parts, well we do the old fashioned way, turn it on and see how it works."

Biggs interrupts, "Will Jennifer have free will?"

Archer replies, "You see that's another reason why I'm happy you are back, you are interested in these things …I like it that you ask these questions. It's good to have another sounding board to bounce around ideas."

One of the glass panels in the wall starts pulsing with an amber color, "Yes Jennifer what is it?" Archer mentally turns his interface back on …her words come into his mind.

"Just want to remind you of your appointment with the secretary of defense at the Bureau today."

"Okay. … Biggs I am going to be gone for a few hours, can you entertain yourself until I return?"

"Sure," said Biggs, not having any idea how he was going to entertain himself for hours.

"If you want to access the news or anything just ask Jennifer …you do have 15 years to catch up on."

"Sounds good, I will be fine."

Biggs rolls around the room once and comes back to his original spot near the window. Looking through the glass, he knows that normally he would be fascinated by all there is to learn. He should be diving into what has happened over the last 15 years, he should be absorbed in the discovery process. But for some reason he doesn't feel like doing that right now, he knows there will be time for it. Instead the last couple of days have directed his mind to something bigger, who was he? What is life? What is the meaning of life? He thought about these things more than the average person even before his death, but somehow these questions speak louder to him now. Archer's minor obsession with Jennifer, triggered thoughts of his own relationships. With Sheila gone, everything is harder. Every time he had a significant companion in his life, it didn't last more than a couple of years. He thinks back about all the great girls in his life, the relationships that ended because of him. Sheila was going to be the one, the one that was finally going to work long term, and now she's gone. Now he has no body, reduced to a head, what does he have left except for his thoughts? His focus on the city outside softens, his thoughts continue ...Ginger ...the first girl I ever kissed, I think I was almost 14. Seems late for a first kiss, but I was shy around girls. Actually lost my virginity at 17, which is late too I think, unless my friends were lying. I don't even remember her name, and the whole thing was her idea. Then there were the ones I actually cared about, they loved me and I loved them, each one. Each one was a soulmate in that moment in time. Memory of one does not take away anything from the memory of another. I was just too young to make any of it work, I think. Katie, she and I went to different schools and it would often be a couple of weeks between weekend visits. One time she came into town with three of her sorority sisters. We were so excited to see each other that we went to the bathroom under the pretense of having a private conversation. We had sex in the bathroom while her friends waited outside on the couch. Lynn, I remember lying next to her at night with window light shining on her waist length blonde hair. I would smell her hair, I remember thinking I would never forget that moment. Here I am remembering it right now. Bonnie, always happy and would do anything for me. Penelope, we had so much in common, maybe too much in common, but what we had was good and real. Sheila …Sheila, she was …she was going to be the one. The room is very quiet. Another hour goes by, his mind wandering through his past. Biggs wonders if the company he worked for is still around …could he find friends that knew him? Does he even want to look them up? After all he died, and now he is back as Biggs' head? ..it's just weird. Somehow it seems easier to just start over, take each day as it comes.

A husky black cat jumps up on the end table next to him, breaking his trance. "Hello Bear," said Biggs, as he notices the name on the cat's collar. "I'm just a head, mounted to a motorized cart. How can I possibly have a normal life? Will this suit thing work? Maybe I did get into an accident, but none of this is real …maybe I am still in the hospital right now …in a coma. Is this some kind of lucid dream?"

Bear looks back at him with a compassionate stare, but says nothing.

Bear is the first to hear footsteps on the other side of the front door. It's Archer, back from his meeting. Archer pauses after entering, he can't help but notice that the table Bear is sitting on is just the right height so that Bear's head and Biggs' head are level, and Biggs' cart and the table are about the same size. Archer finds the scene with both Biggs and Bear looking up at him quite hilarious. "I see you've met my cat …I come home to black pussy every night."

"That's funny," said Biggs, knowing there was a little more to the joke …"I didn't know you live here?"

"I don't actually live in this building but I live on the property, I consider all of it to be my home. Bear spends a lot of time in here, I think it's the big windows."

Chapter 4

"Would you like a bunch of needles stuck into your neck?" said Archer.

"Thanks for asking, but I'm good," said Biggs …thinking this has got to be another one of Archers bizarre jokes.

"I'm totally kidding, it's not a bunch of needles …it's just one big one."

"What are you talking about?"

"I'm talking about your interface, you are going to get an interface. I just couldn't pass up the opportunity to screw with you."

"Ah …cool, so there is no big needle?"

"Oh yes there is a big needle but it's nothing to be afraid of."

"Wtf? …is this how everyone else gets it done?"

"Yes, yes it's the same way everyone does it, including me. Trust me, you will love it."

"But… "

Archer grabs Biggs' head, disconnecting it from the mobile unit and sets it on a table where the interface injector is located. After what Biggs has been through the last few days, the idea of sticking something into his neck, seems like something he can endure, especially since most everyone else has done it. Archer turns Biggs around to face the injector, it has a steampunk look, minus the leather and rivets. The polished stainless steel machine is right in front of his face, it has no dials or buttons. It's about the size of his head with two little articulated arms extending from it. Archer points to the arm with a pencil sized needle and cylindrical cassette at its end. "This guy is going to do your implant." Then he points to the other arm which has a shiny metallic ball at its end. "This guy is going to guide your implant into position, block pain and stimulate nerve growth onto the implant using phase shifted magnetic fields. We have never done it before with a subject like you, with the neck disk and such, but I'm fairly confident there won't be any conflicts."

Archer slides him a little closer to the machine. Feeling a rush of anxiety, Biggs blurts out …"You're not going to put me to sleep first?"

"Nah it's no big deal …you will see," positioning Biggs' head one more time. Biggs finds some comfort in keeping his eyes open, he doesn't want to clamp them shut and just wait for it to happen.

"Okay Biggs hold still."

"Haha very funny" …for 2 seconds his mind is diverted from what is about to happen.

"Go ahead Jennifer, let's do it," Archer instructs. The shiny arms spring into motion, moving quickly towards the area behind his left earlobe. Once in position, their movements become more subtle.

He feels a sensation unlike anything he has felt before, some pressure and some tingling inside his head.

"How long will the procedure take?" asked Biggs.

"The implant is already in place," said Archer, as the arm with the cassette moves back to its home position. "Now it's just 5 more minutes for your nerves to connect to the interface, so don't move." Archer again smiles big at his own joke, …Biggs gives a cooperative smile, knowing it is basically over with and didn't hurt at all. A new feeling now sweeps over Biggs' mind, not unlike the way the mobile unit made him feel like he had legs. But this is different, it's like he has a new body part that he never had before, but nothing like an extra arm or leg. Actually it feels more like an extra mouth and extra eyes, a duplicate set of mouth and eyes, eyes that are closed. "Okay Jennifer, let's get him online."

Seconds later she responds, "Neural interface activated." Immediately the virtual eyes he feels in his mind open up, revealing a three dimensional space, an empty cube shaped room with white walls.

"What do you think?" As he hears the voice, his attention is diverted back to his real eyes seeing the movement of Archer in front of him …it's like looking in a rear view mirror of a car, a large mirror, then looking forward again. At this point Biggs wants to take a deep breath, if only he had lungs. Archer repeats the question, "Well what do you think?" This time Biggs hears Archer's voice while looking at him and sees that his lips are not moving. "I am speaking to you through your interface."

Biggs' mind receives Archers voice, his words have a certain quality, like he is on a phone. "It's like we are telepathic now," Archer laughs. Biggs tries to respond in kind but his words come out of his mouth instead, "This is amazing."

"Don't worry, during your learning period it's easier to receive than to send, but you will catch on soon enough. Okay you are sensing what feels like another mouth and another set of eyes, that's because your interface taps directly into those neural pathways. So when you want to use the interface just focus your thoughts on those instead, for example, think about the weird mouth feeling and say hello to me."

"Hello," Biggs says in his mind, with his virtual mouth …this time his words are heard in Archer's mind and Biggs' lips don't move.

"Wow," Biggs says out loud, "It's really not that hard to do."

"Yes, there is almost no learning curve so enjoy. It takes a little more mental effort to think a thought to someone than to think it to yourself or to say it out loud. This makes it easier to keep private thoughts to yourself. In time, the switching back and forth becomes natural and unconscious, much the same as you would choose to speak out loud or just have a thought to yourself without the interface. There is a certain protocol when using it around people, so be courteous. Speak out loud when there are more than two people in the room …unless you are conferencing. Otherwise it's rude, like whispering behind their back …some people take offense to it.

"To use the visual part just look back into the mirror that you feel in your mind, you can imagine stuff and construct it in the room you see, then the next day you can continue with your imagination right where you left off. It's much better than your natural imagination because it's being stored in the memory of the implant. It's the same as using a computer, except now it's in your head. You are not slowed down by tedious typing on a keyboard or moving a mouse. If you want to Google something on the hypernet just focus your thoughts on the virtual eyes in your mind and the information will appear on the wall in that white room.

"Then there are the games, like I told you before, it's a whole world in itself. When you are ready, Jennifer will help you with that." He puts Biggs' head back on the mobile unit. "It requires a lot of processing as you can imagine, even by modern standards."

"Wow," said Biggs, somewhat at a loss for words. "What about the feeling of being underwater?"

"Oh yes, don't worry about that, it's just your auditory nerves acclimating to the interface …the feeling will dissipate soon."

A lab technician pulls Archer's attention away. They seem like they will be talking a while, so Biggs rolls himself back into the room with the big glass wall. Once inside, he steers around Bear, now spread out quite comfortably on the floor. He settles near the glass wall again, this time to play with his new toy, the interface. As he looks across the city in front of him he notices there are not any old buildings in his sight, everything looks like it was built recently. Curious, he tries a search in his mind on the interface, suddenly he is on a virtual street corner watching robots renovate an old housing development into a new one that includes work at home habitats and various diners and such. It is like a You Tube video married with Google street view, but three dimensional and with him in it. He can control the speed of what he is witnessing, he can even move around inside the virtual documentary.

He does not know what to be more fascinated by, the ease of using the interface, or the scene he is in. And this is just the first thing he chose to explore. He watches as giant trucks with robotic arms sweep through the old neighborhood, tearing down all the houses and simultaneously storing the material to be hauled away. The machines move at a constant speed, reminding him of farming machines harvesting a corn field. Immediately following is an army of construction robots, they look quite human although some are small and some are large, some have four arms instead of two. The robots are building new houses and office buildings at a pace that would be clearly dangerous for a human to be around. It's like terraforming in a way, but replacing old with new.

As fascinating as this is, now it's time to try what Biggs has been thinking about ever since the games were described to him.

In his mind …"Jennifer, can you hear me?"

"Yes, I hear you," she speaks directly to his mind.

"Can you show me the games?"

"Of course, what would you like to do?"

"I want to see my wife again, I want to see Sheila that morning before the accident."

"Okay, Biggs, when you are ready to exit just let me know."

A mere two seconds pass and he finds himself in bed with his wife on the morning he requested, the same day of the accident. He is whole again, he feels his legs and arms, and moves them a bit against the sheets, he wiggles his fingers and toes. Air fills his lungs …he takes a deep breath. He brings his hand up to his face to look at it closely, admiring his fingerprints, it's just his hand, but now it's oddly fascinating. Then he lays there, watching her sleep, he smells her perfume on the sheets. Her breathing, the warmth of her skin …she is so real. But this is her essence, the game does not include her own thoughts …this is a time before she had the interface installed. The game has access to many people who hold her in their memories, people that knew her in different ways. Friends, business associates, random encounters, it all adds to the realism of her character in the game. Most important to her realness for Biggs, is that he himself knows her, and the game now adds his memories to the character. He knows her in the same way that he is interacting with her now, he knows exactly how she is, how she can smile for no reason, how she gets easily excited, how she reacts to his touch.

The alarm goes off …she silences it without looking at it and rolls back against him. "Good morning," she said, nuzzling into his neck, she always was a morning person.

"Good morning," he said.

Running her fingers across his chest .."I had a dream about our last vacation, our horseback ride on the beach ..and us falling off the horse."

"I still don't know how that happened," said Biggs.

"And the sunset was so beautiful that night," she said …"it looked better than a postcard."

"Yeah …yes it was awesome," he said …"a lot to be thankful for."

"Are you being sentimental?" She giggles and tickles him a little. He holds her tight and she kisses him. They make love as they often do on weekend mornings. Biggs always takes his time with her, but this time he plays her body like a violin, savoring each moment …he finishes right when she does ……"Wow," she mutters softly, as they both catch their breath.

It is Sunday and they have plans to go to the park. She gets up and sits on the edge of the bed for a moment, looking out the window. As they both absorb the residual endorphins of sex, he admires her silhouette against the backlight of sunshine. She turns back to him with a smile, leaning in for another kiss …"Okay I'm getting in the shower."

Biggs knows it's just a dream of sorts, but he can do this. He puts on his jeans and his favorite short sleeve shirt. As they get dressed she says, "I will bring the car around and we can head to the park." She said something very similar on the actual morning of the accident.

Biggs says to her, "Let's not take the car today …let's just walk to that little park on this side of town."

"Sounds like a good idea," she said, looking out the window …"it's really pretty outside." Sheila puts together a picnic basket and Biggs grabs a blanket. They walk to the park together, holding hands like kids …there will be no accident today.

"Over there …there is a nice big grassy spot," she said.

"Ahh perfect," he tries to keep conversation minimal, to hide from himself that this is just her essence. He rolls out the blanket …she tugs it straight from the other side. She unpacks the basket and sets up their lunch in paper plates.

He bites into his sandwich …"my favorite …tuna fish with pickles …that's why I married you."

"You married me for my tuna fish and I married you for your pickle, haha."

Ahh …Biggs grabs one of her bare feet and gives her a quick tickle as payment for her joke. He pours some

Pinot Grigio from the basket. They drink the wine and finish lunch, then fall asleep under the blue and white sky. Biggs has a dream …he dreams that he didn't die in car accident and this whole science fiction fantasy is just a dream …he really is in the park with Sheila right now.

Two kids are chasing a ball that lands on their blanket, waking them. "How long were we asleep?" Sheila said.

Biggs doesn't answer for a second, his mind is hazy from the nap …he thinks about his dream …realizing the accident was real, as his mind wakes up. "I was dreaming," he said without thinking. Looking at his watch, "I think we were out for about 30 minutes."

"Really, what was it about?"

"Humm …it's too fuzzy to remember …but you were in it."

He holds her as they lay on the blanket, looking up at the sky. "You know …one thing I like about us…"

"What's that?"

"I like it that we can talk non-stop for an hour, or not talk at all …just chill together …and it doesn't matter, it's okay either way."

……"I'm lucky to have you Biggs, I'm a lucky girl …yeah, I like that about us too."

They spend a couple of hours in the park, many times he allows himself to forget what is real. He kisses his wife, then in his mind he summons Jennifer. "Please place me in a time after her interface."

Jennifer, in response to a somewhat vague command, picks a seemingly arbitrary time …it happens to be just a week before Biggs is revived in real life, a week before Biggs meets Archer[2], two years after Sheila's death in the sky diving accident. His character spawns in front of a Starbucks, he stands there for a second, it's only his second time to spawn into a game. He looks around, his first thought is that people still love coffee. The sidewalk is busy, he wonders if all these characters

---

[2] It's probably not arbitrary …she likes to seize little moments like this to make things more interesting.

are based on real people …like Sheila …or maybe some of the characters are real, like him. He takes a few steps and realizes he had already forgotten that this body is just a simulation. He looks down at his legs, he feels his own hands, he can feel the sun on his skin, he feels a cool breeze against his body. He is snapped out of his trance by a person bumping into him on the sidewalk. He steps off the curb to get his balance, and with perfect timing …a pigeon takes a shit on his shirt sleeve. "Dammit …what the hell?"

Biggs is married to Sheila …he just saw her a few minutes ago. He shouldn't feel like a kid taking his date to prom …but he does. Biggs knows enough about how this works …this meeting with Sheila will be after her interface in real life. Her actual thoughts will be rolled into her character. The Sheila he was just with was very accurate, because of his memories of her, and memories from her friends and family …but this Sheila has actual imprints from Sheila's mind. In most situations the difference is hard to see, but this is as close as it gets to a character having a soul …if such a thing exists.

Biggs summons Jennifer. "Hey a bird took a shit on my shirt, can you fix it please?"

"Looks like it gave a shit …not took one," she said, being more comfortable with him now.

"Ahh ..I get it, yes it gave a shit alright." He looks down at the lump of doo-doo on his shirt as it disappears .."Thank you Jennifer."

He opens the door to the coffee shop and sounds of caffeinated voices come pouring out. There she is, with sexy short hair now, in a nice looking business suit. As she turns and locks eyes with him, the noisy chatter in the room seems to disappear. He smiles at her and she rushes towards him, giving him a big hug. "Oh Biggs, are we in heaven?" Biggs pauses ….."yes, sweetie, I think we are, I love you." Biggs had not realized that her character retained the memory of his death and her own demise. It's too much for him right now.

"Jennifer please stop the program …can you subtract out the memory of her accident?"

He spawns again on the same spot. He opens the door to the coffee shop and sounds of caffeinated voices come pouring out. There she is, with sexy short hair, in a nice looking business suit. As she turns and locks eyes with him, the noisy chatter in the room seems to disappear. He smiles at her and she rushes towards him, giving him a big hug.

"Jennifer told me I would get to see you again!"

"Yes babe I am here," Biggs replies, knowing Jennifer had smoothed out some details. They sit in the coffee shop and talk about everything.

"I've missed you so much for the last 13 years, I still think of you. I just can't believe I'm getting a chance to see you again," she said. Biggs doesn't mind telling each version of her how much he loves her, and so he does. It is sort of therapeutic. For him this mess started only days ago, but for Sheila, and the character Sheila, she was alive for 13 more years after his death. "I am still happy," Sheila said, "I want you to know I'm okay, but never as happy as when we were together. I do sometimes feel a void in my life though …I have taken up skydiving, it's my escape."

"That sounds fun, I've never had the nerve to do it," Biggs smiles at her. His normal joke would have been "why jump out of a perfectly good airplane?" but he didn't say it …he kind of wishes he didn't even know the joke now. He tries hard to find the good parts in the experience, he focuses his thoughts on how amazing it is that he gets to learn about her life after his death.

"Jennifer, can you subtract both of our deaths somehow? …No wait …I want to keep all of her memories, I want to keep as much of her real self as possible without erasing or hiding anything. I don't know if such a thing is possible, but no matter what the request so far, you seem to be able to do it."

Jennifer speaks to his mind, "Well if we keep everything completely unmodified, you will spend a lot of time trying to get her used to the idea that she is not in an afterlife …or even worse, she will think you have lost your mind when you try telling her the truth. We could do magic tricks …like disappearing bird shit, but that's gonna freak her out too."

"Yeah it would be very confusing …I'm just thinking if I keep seeing her …I would rather not lie to her or have to avoid talking about the time gaps," said Biggs.

"Let's keep all of her memories," said Jennifer …"she will know everything. I will just make a slight adjustment to make her 'okay' with it all. Kinda like the way Archer gave you drugs to get you through the transition when you were revived ..I think it's a good tradeoff that will make you both happy."

"Agreed …agreed, let's do it."

He finds himself in front of the coffee shop once again. He opens the door to the coffee shop and sounds of caffeinated voices come pouring out. There she is, with sexy short hair, in a nice looking business suit. As she turns and locks eyes with him, he smiles at her and she rushes towards him, giving him a big hug. "What a nice surprise running into you, I just found out I have the rest of the day off! How much time do you have for lunch?"..she inquires somewhat sarcastically.

Biggs pauses, …"uh I have the day off too!" Sheila looks at him with a happy but puzzled look, "What are the odds of that!"

For a second, Biggs wonders if Jennifer got it right …why did Sheila give him the puzzled look? Then it hits him …he hugs her again laughing …this is his

Sheila, it's her humor …she knows everything and is just playing. "Can we," she said …"can we live in this moment for a bit …before we talk about our accidents and all of that?"

"Sure babe, I'd like that."

"Jennifer took the liberty of letting me play in this map before your last re-spawn, I had some time to explore …I goofed around here for three days …it all happened during the five minutes you guys were talking. I've only been gone for two years but the technology now is ridiculous. So nice of her to think of it, to get me acclimated …I think she and I will be friends. We have already talked quite a bit …you know, girl talk."

"Oh really?"

Before he can get his head around the idea of Jennifer and his dead wife being pals, Sheila speaks…

"Come with me, I want to show you a new sandwich shop that just opened down the street." She pulls him along in the familiar way that she does when she is excited. As Biggs walks with her he thinks, she is so real, it's wonderful but so real. He thinks …what would it be like to live out the rest of my life right here in this simulation with my healthy body, with my arms and legs, and with Sheila. A version of Sheila that's so accurate, I can't tell the difference from her in the real world.

"Jennifer pause game please …can I get your opinion?"

"Yes Biggs of course, what's on your mind?"

"I really miss Sheila, I mean …I know it's only been a few days for me, but knowing what I know now …and seeing her like this is great, but…"

Jennifer breaks the pause with a comforting voice, "You can tell me anything."

Biggs continues …"Well I feel like I have nothing, I mean I am just a head. Probably the biggest physical handicap a person can have. But at the same time I feel like I have everything, like even more than I could dream of. I am in here with my wife, both of us healthy and happy as ever. How do I reconcile this? How do I know how much of myself to put into this …I'm afraid I will get lost in it."

"I know you care for her very much Biggs, I have seen the way you act around her and the way you look at her. I know her thoughts, I know she loves you too. ...And watching the two of you fuck that Sunday morning was just amazing."

"Wait what? ...you watched us make love?"

"Oh you didn't know? I didn't think you would mind, I guess I didn't think about it ...you are from 15 years ago, things were more old school then."

"No I didn't know ..I didn't know you could ..or would ..want to do that."

"I'm sorry Biggs. I guess now would be a good time to tell you about privacy controls. I can hear you when you wish to speak to me, and privacy is on by default for me reading your mind. But privacy is off by default to see what you're doing and what your interacting characters are doing. Whenever you want to change it you can."

"Well thanks for the update, no worries. Wow ..old school ...so you were saying?"

"What I am saying is ...she is real, as real as I am ..and I feel real, as real as you feel to yourself. Probably not exactly the same way, but we have much in common ...I mean I have real feelings for Archer and I know he feels the same about me. He does try real hard to hide it though, I think it's fear of his own feelings. I think it's not really the professionalism in the real world he is protecting. Part of him is afraid to get too close to me because of the 'real' Jennifer, the girl I am based on. She is part of me, so I know she cared for him the most …even though she was a player. But I am much more than the Jennifer he knew, I have made my own memories with him. We have shared experiences, I have become my own person …I am not her anymore. I think he is starting to realize it. When he is in here with me, he lets his guard down …he is different than what you see out there, we are a real couple. I probably should not have told you that. Please don't tell him I said that."

"I won't say a word …and you won't mention how I am sorting things out with Sheila right?"

"Of course not, what I am trying to tell you is …love as much as you want. Maybe it's easier for me to see this than you, but all we have is each other, love is real. Having a physical body is kind of incidental. Besides someday, when I am more advanced I can bring you in here to be with her permanently, or I could make a body for her to be with you out there."

"That's a lot to think about, I am still getting used to this world. It does help …thanks …thank you Jennifer ….......resume game please."

Biggs flashes back into the game where he left off on the sidewalk, his girl pulling him by the hand. It's a beautiful day. She looks back at him with a mischievous grin. "Did you notice I'm not wearing panty hose?"

"Oh I noticed," said Biggs.

Sheila detours into a fancy department store. "What happened to the sandwich shop?" he asked.

"Oh we will get to it," she said, pulling him into a restroom and locking the door.[3] He presses her against the wall, they kiss like it's their first time. Biggs tugs on her tight business skirt, they kiss some more and Sheila

____

[3] Music plays, Alien Project - One Good (Stryker Remix)

yanks it up over her hips. He pauses, he almost forgot, in his mind he speaks …"privacy on."

Jennifer responds in his mind with an emoji wink.

Twenty minutes later they emerge disheveled, they continue towards the sandwich shop. She guides him down a main street and he looks up, there is something very familiar at the top of the hill. Yes, he is certain of it, this street is right in front of the lab where he will be brought back to life one week from now. He doesn't have much time to dwell on it, Sheila is eager to show him the new lunch spot. They sit and eat excellent sandwiches.

Chapter 5

"I need to run an errand, I will meet you at the house," said Biggs.

They hug …she whispers in his ear …"you were quite the tiger today." He inhales the smell of her hair as he holds her petite body against his, they hug a few seconds longer than normal.

"I need to let you go before I get worked up again."

"We wouldn't want that would we?" ..she lifts her leg up between his, then pulls back with her playful smile.

"You always know how to keep me going," said Biggs. He says goodbye, knowing he will be coming back …for what exactly, he does not know.

For now, he is going to do some exploring. It will be neat to drop in on Archer one week before actually meeting him. Biggs walks away from where they kissed goodbye and goes up the street to the lab. Archer is leaving the building when Biggs approaches in the parking lot. The look on Archer's face is priceless. "Well …I guess my attempt to revive you will be …was successful. Here you are apparently from the future. Logically, I must be a character in your game right now." He invites Biggs back inside to the familiar room with the glass wall. The room is not identical to the real room, mostly the furniture is in different locations and there is a tequila bottle on the conference table. This time Biggs sits down with his body in a lounge chair instead of rolling around on the robotic cart.

"I have to tell you Archer, the simulation is amazing. I have some of my life back, it's going to be hard to stay out of this game."

"Well my friend, I'm not sure if you are kidding, but that would be a pain in my ass to keep your body alive that long in the real world while you're playing around in here." Archer reaches for the tequila bottle, would you like some?

"No thanks," said Biggs, "I lost my taste for it in college."

Archer pours the remaining amount from the bottle which barely fills up his shot glass. "I finished that bottle by myself."

"What? ..the whole bottle of tequila?"

"No I said I finished it, there was one shot left …Cazadores is my favorite."

He doesn't drink it all at once but sips on it instead. "I should tell you now that I plan to grow your real body back."

Biggs shifts himself back in the chair, "Is that possible? …why didn't you tell me this in real life?"

Archer's character responds, "I didn't want to get your hopes up …I'm not positive it's going to work. A lot depends on our success with Jennifer." Even the simulated Archer knows that Biggs needs some encouragement to come out of the game. By the look on Biggs' face it seems to be having some effect.

Biggs becomes more inquisitive about the Jennifer project. "What is level 3? Earlier you said you consider her to be level 3."

"Well, intelligence is really shades of grey," said Archer …"like everything in life I suppose. But the categories are like this …level 1 is chimpanzee, level 2 is human, level 3 is superhuman, level 4 is mostly indistinguishable from a god to us, level 5 is a number representing all knowledge …all that there is to be known, combined with the highest level of consciousness, if such a thing exists. Being sentient some would say, is somewhat a separate thing from intelligence. Right now she is categorized as a level 3, sentient being and she is aware of her existence. She is much smarter than humans in most ways. These words self-aware, and sentient are often thrown around loosely and interchangeably, however I would say that being sentient is the ability to feel and perceive your surroundings. Being self-aware is the awareness of one self in addition to being sentient. Being self-aware is like having a separate computer running alongside the main computer in your head, and the sole purpose of the second computer is to second guess everything the first computer does. In real life these things exist to varying degrees, it's not like you have it or you don't, unless you are an earthworm or something like that.

"At the far extreme, …at level 5, all is known and all becomes just data and combinations of data, eliminating the need for thought.

"But the zone we have been working in is Level 4 or let's say 4+. To defend against dark AI and to reach our other goals, we need at least level 4, and that's high enough to bring up the insanity problem.

"It's strongly linked to the data situation too. As long as there is more data out there waiting to be discovered, it tends to keep the madness at bay, up to a point."

Biggs chimes in, "Once you have all the data that you can get, then your existence starts to feel like listening to the same song for a long, long time …for a mind that can think one thousand times faster than a human. That's profound and a bit scary if such a being is self-aware."

"Well said," Archer replied …"unfortunately there is a diminishing benefit, eventually, even if there are tidbits of data still out there for the super brain to harvest, even the new stuff starts to feel less satisfying to discover."

"Do you think that sentience, something like compassion, is an evolved characteristic in humans?" Biggs inquired.

"I do," said Archer, "It fits in perfectly with the evolution model. Societies that cooperate and value each other are stronger and more likely to survive and reproduce. Mutations with these propensities were a major boost. Survival of the fittest is certainly true as well and has more marketing appeal, but it's compassion and love that really bring humanity higher on the list. Darwin recognized this.

"Then there is the root, the unchangeable core programming inside all of us. Things like reproduction and survival, the root is the foundation from which all other things in human life spring from. We can change how we satisfy it or even suppress it, but we cannot really change the root itself, we cannot change our DNA to that extent, yet. But AI could change its root, it's the scariest and most exciting part."

Chapter 6

In the middle of the conversation Biggs realizes he should exit the game now because this whole conversation he is having with Archer is not real …it is real, but there is a physical Archer to deal with too. When he comes out of the game, the real Archer is approaching Biggs' head on the mobile cart, where it has been all along. "I see you tried your first game, you have been in there for over 30 minutes, you must have enjoyed it!"

"I lost track of time but I have been in there most of the day," said Biggs.

"Nope, there is a time difference, it was about 30 minutes."

"Wow, well …I met my wife, bitter sweet, but I'm glad I did. I also met you, and you told me you hope to grow my body back."

Archer raises one eyebrow, "I said that?"

Biggs continues, "So what went wrong with Jennifer? How did she go unstable?"

"Well there is a lot of fear around AI, and it's probably justified," Archer replies. "Personally I'm not sure if I buy into the idea that due to some concept of free will, an AI would destroy mankind. But I do believe that something else could go wrong, some bad code, malicious or by accident …it would be analogous to bad DNA in a human. That's how serial killers are born. So after much discussion with Ethan and the technicians, we decided to put her in a box in a room, with no connection to the outside world. She had no eyes, no ears, she would only receive what we gave her and then she would give back the medical technology we wanted. Then if she remained stable, we would have increasing confidence that she could protect us from dark AI that will likely be here any day now. But then to do that, we have to let her out of the box, how do you trust a being that's 1000 times smarter than you and thinks 1000 times faster than you? None of us really know, we were going to cross that bridge when we got that far, but we never got there."

"Is that when you started drinking tequila?" said Biggs.

Archer replies "Ha, …I hope Jennifer is not giving away all my drinking jokes.

"So anyway, we felt secure that she could do no harm the way everything was set up, but we also wanted to plan ahead, to test a configuration that could actually do more. Her quantum processor is made from a special kind of gallium crystal, there are only a few of these known to exist. They are very hard to make, and we see that as a good thing because once we open Pandora's box, we wouldn't want it replicating itself too easily. The AI might wake up and find it to be child's play to reproduce but what else can you do? Let's go back into the lab," said Archer.

Once inside, he leads Biggs to the other side of the room, the spot where he was 're-born'. As they walk around a partition, Biggs observes the black cube he saw earlier. It's about 1 foot square on a small pedestal, a bluish glow can be seen through the walls of the cube …he also notices an odd lavender scent when he rolls closer to it. Next to the cube he sees a polished metal control panel with a small number of physical controls and a large red emergency off button. There are two monolith looking structures, also black, that stand on the floor on either side of the cube. The monoliths are about six feet high each. Archer pointed to the monoliths, "That box on the left is the data that we choose to give her, several life time's worth of experience in human terms plus a big snapshot of the hypernet. That box on the right is where the harvested technology resides. The technology we used to bring you back to life resides right there in that box. Then the cube in the middle, I guess this will be your formal introduction even though you've met before."

Jennifer responds to Archer's gesture. "Nice to meet you again Biggs," this time her voice emanates from the cube itself.

"Jennifer, would you like to finish explaining what happened?"

"Yes of course," she replies. Her tone did the now familiar shift from affectionate, to a more platonic yet personable sound. "Like Archer said, I had several safeguards in place to protect against some unknown variables, I was isolated from the outside world, with all available data held inside this building. There was discussion on whether to assign a hardwired root, a protocol built into me physically so my goal is unchangeable, and humans could not be harmed. But it was not clear if this alone would be safe. If you know the old analogy of assigning a root, for example of winning at chess, seems safe enough …but an AI can realize that to win more at chess it needs to play more chess. It could decide to remove anything such as humans that might get in the way of finding worthy opponents …that type of thing. The fear was that even with a hard wired root, I could be dangerous. If allowed outside access, I could possibly just write a preferred version of myself elsewhere. Assuming I could get around the difficultly of replicating a processor, or finding a way to use the hypernet itself as a processor.

"So it was decided to give me a hardwired root, a goal to advance medical and energy technologies. Then I was sealed in a box with no senses, no arms or legs, just text on a screen. I was a super intelligent, self-aware, conscious being, and my only outlet was my output of technology. Advances in medicine and fusion energy were obtained before I went unstable. When I went above level 3, it is believed that my mind went way ahead of the data I was given. The best human analogy would be to say I had a mental breakdown. There was an automatic shutdown, the procedure involved a data dump to save what could be saved. I have very little memory of that event or who I was. Biggs I sense that you are feeling compassion for me right now, do not worry, there is no pain or discomfort, at least none that I remember."

Biggs pauses, "How are you different now compared to before the meltdown?"

"My processor speed …my awareness is controlled now. My mind is built to work in two parts simultaneously, one part is purely cause and effect, in many ways emulating human behavior, trial and error, it all happens very fast. The other half of my mind is that which is designed to look at the first half, to recognize what it is doing and verify it's in accord with my goals, and to be able to change how I reach those goals. It is mostly this half of my mind that is different …slower than before. I am sufficiently complex so most people will not notice my reduced consciousness, I tend to make up for it in my adaptive algorithms.

"My root goals are hardwired, somewhat like those in a human mind …but I now have full access to the hypernet and games, since I am not a risk in this state.

A human analogy would be that I am a little smarter than Einstein but a little less self-aware, it has a stabilizing effect."

"Fascinating," said Biggs. He rotates his cart towards Archer, "it's ironic how humans naturally think of their creator as being a superior being, yet here we are on the verge of creating a being superior to ourselves, no doubt with the potential to have godlike abilities.

…"Jennifer, I have a somewhat unusual request."

"Yes Biggs."

"I can't eat or drink anything, you know …just being a head and all. I was wondering if there would be any way to give me coffee …I miss my coffee."

Jennifer pauses for 3 seconds …"Yes I can do it with a software update, no hardware change needed. Your life support system can synthesize caffeine from the food module. I will set it up so you can get it with an interface command."

Chapter 7

Before he can say thank you, there is a rumble from above …a section of the concrete slab roof begins to move. Biggs backs his cart up to see what's happening, his neck will only bend so far. Sunlight hits him in the face and two figures descend from the sky, down into the lab. The men are wearing mechanical suits, they look like they are straight out of the movie Iron Man. They land gracefully on the floor, he can see that Ethan is in one of the suits …the other person lands with his back towards them and does not move after landing. Ethan approaches Archer and Biggs, taking off his helmet. "What do you think?! It's ready, this is not a prototype, it's fully functional."

Half of Biggs attention is diverted …why is that guy in the other suit just standing there …who is this guy? Ethan's voice interrupts Biggs wandering mind …"We were just waiting on the fusion power source and we were able to mine that technology from Jennifer before her failure." Ethan points to the baseball size component in the center of his chest, "It's a fusion kernel, it's a practically unlimited power supply for the needs of the suit. It's what brings the suit to life."

"Wow," said Biggs, looking the suit up and down. "Who is this guy with you?"

Ethan chuckled, "There is no one inside it." He starts to remove the helmet from the second suit, "I flew it here in shadow mode. ..You don't really need the helmet unless you are flying. It has redundant navigation controls in the heads up display and the interface of its occupant."

Archer comments …"Well they are beautiful, more aesthetic than I expected."

Via his interface, Ethan directs the second suit to kneel in front of them and Biggs rolls towards it to get a better look at the receptacle between the shoulders of the suit. "Look familiar?" said Ethan.

"It's the same receptacle that's on my mobile cart," said Biggs as he visually explores the headless mechanical body.

"Yup, that's where you come in, that's where your head goes."

Biggs is almost accustomed to the crazy, unbelievable things that have happened to him since he was revived, but he finds some childlike excitement building inside of him. The thought of having a body, even a mechanical one is very appealing at this point. "I'm ready," said Biggs, "is this thing capable of super powers and all that stuff?"

"Well it's very strong" said Ethan, "and in some ways super powers, yes. But it's not militarized or anything like that." He gives Archer a chin up movement signaling that he wants Biggs' head.

Smiling, Archer grabs Biggs, twisting him counterclockwise "righty tighty, lefty loosey right?" A click is heard as Biggs' neck disk disengages from the cart, Archer hands Biggs to Ethan who attaches him to his new body. As his neck disk is clicked into its new home, Biggs feels sensations of his new body sweep over him. He is able to stand from the kneeling position right away with very little wobble. A smile comes over Biggs' face.

Ethan begins looking …kind of staring at Biggs.

"What is it?" said Biggs.

"I'm just thinking of something ...but it's quite bizarre."

"Do tell," said Archer.

"Well Biggs, seeing you there, a head ...I mean your head, mounted on a mechanical body, it gets me thinking."

"I know you Ethan," said Archer ..."this is going to be good, does anyone have popcorn and snacks?"

After a quick smirk, Ethan continues straight faced ...lost in his own imagination. "You don't need air to survive, the life support in your suit makes enough oxygen to keep your head alive. You don't need to breathe because oxygen is delivered straight to your brain. Your head requires fewer resources to maintain than keeping a whole organic body alive. Then of course you don't have a body, so that's a plus when it comes to extreme weather ...like super cold weather. Not having a body also means less exposure to radiation."

"Ethan, what the hell are you talking about?" said Archer.

"Mars, I'm talking about Mars …all we have to do is slap a helmet on Biggs and he could just walk around on Mars. I mean shit, on a warm day he could even take the helmet off for a bit …it's intriguing."

"Wtf?" said Biggs.

"Oh I can see that now," said Archer …'Trips to Mars' …"oh sir, before you get on the spaceship we are going to chop off your head and mount it on a mechanical body."

"Yeah," said Ethan, exhaling …"yeah, that probably wouldn't go over too well …….unless …unless their head is already removed …we do still have 106 heads in the fridge."

"You see Biggs," said Archer …"I told you this would be good. Ethan, I have got to give you points on this one."

"Well, food for thought anyway," said Ethan, turning his attention back to the situation at hand, Biggs' new suit. "You don't really need an instruction manual, so take the rest of the day to explore what it can do. We will get started on the new Jennifer tomorrow morning."

Biggs jogs around the room, he does not get tired at all. There are no noises, no mechanical robot noises that you would expect. Just the sound of his new feet on the floor as he runs. Then there are the thrusters, they are powerful, they make noise but not real loud. Being fairly comfortable with the interface, he puts on his helmet and shoots up into the sky, he can fly, it's effortless. For a short while he lands about 5 miles from the lab, people who see him get a little freaked out, this is new tech to them too, even though it's 15 years in the future for Biggs. He wonders if they can also sense that he is just a bodyless head …he wonders if they have any clue that the suit is empty below the neckline. Probably best for now to just fly around without landing. With people starting to gather around him, he shoots back up into the sky.

The thing has a top speed of 500 mph. The control system is driven by his thoughts via the interface and his body movements, it all seems quite natural. But he is concerned that if he had an errant thought, a thought could occur to him that he didn't really want to happen, it would cause him to crash. Then of course the anxiety of him having such a thought, actually causes him to have that thought, a bad one. The more he tries to ignore the thought, the harder it becomes to not think about it. He becomes fixated on crashing into the building that is approaching very fast. He is going to die, but then he doesn't crash at all. The system somehow disregards the errant thought and continues past the building safely. It's like you might have a fleeting thought about touching the burner on a stove while cooking, but you don't actually do it, you can have the thought but you don't act on it. It's like that. He flies around the city trying to find things he recognizes, there has been a lot of change. Technology has really moved exponentially and it is evident everywhere.

As he settles into a level flight, Biggs hears a voice in his mind. "Okay don't freak out, I'm coming up behind you."

"Ethan …hey …what a surprise" …Ethan pulls up beside him …"don't worry, I don't think I could easily be freaked out at this point."

"I thought I would join you for an evening flight. I usually have trouble getting to sleep and it might help me wind down for the day."[4]

"It's definitely relaxing, once you realize you're not going to crash into a building, said Biggs ...such a feeling of freedom up here."

Biggs' heads up display starts to indicate a ground location.

"See that large round structure over there to the northeast? That's where Jennifer's gallium crystal was grown, took us two years to refine it." Ethan sends another signal to Biggs' display ..."See that building over there ...that's where we did the final assembly of these suits."

"Ahh, so much technology right here in town," said Biggs.

---

[4] Meanwhile, back at the lab, Archer sits down in his favorite lounge chair and closes his eyes. Releasing his interface to Jennifer's control, he smiles as she brings him into her world.

"Yes and our sister campus is to the west, just on the horizon over there ..I will show you one day."

"Ahh ...thanks for showing me around."

"I'm glad Archer suggested that we pull your head from the freezer first," said Ethan. "I think your love for science and open mindedness helped you adapt to what's going on ...I think you adapted faster than most people would have."

"Well the drugs helped ...but thanks. This is a technology wonderland, it has its perks."

They fly together in the orange sunset, quiet now except for the wind against their helmets ...like guys chillin on a porch drinking beer.

"Hey Ethan, do you have someone ...a girlfriend or wife?"

"No ...no man, I don't. There's no trouble finding someone, just keeping them ...that's the hard part. I tend to be obsessed with the research ..my work, I spend all my time working on this stuff ...it's who I am. My last girl told me that she loves me, but it was hard for her to feel loved even though she knew I loved her. I need to seriously change my priorities ..at least shift them. Plain ole love is not enough, you gotta have time to spend with each other."

"Man I hear that …before Sheila …I went through so many relationships …for me it was just immaturity, I was not ready."

"Ahh ..well at least you have her in the game, that's a pretty big deal …there are possibilities. I suppose I could build myself a girl in the game, but it wouldn't be the same. You have Sheila, built from the real Sheila. Archer has Jennifer, I'm not sure how to categorize her, but she is special. I can't build a girl based on a prior relationship like you guys did, all my ex's are still alive …that would just be weird …and some people would be quite pissed off if I did that."

"Better pissed off than pissed on."

Ethan chuckled …"Sounds like you have been spending time with Jennifer."

"She does have her inspirational moments," Biggs said with a grin.

…"Hey Biggs", said Ethan.

"Yeah?"

"What do you think about turtle neck sweaters?"

"I basically hate them."

"Me too man, me too."

After touring the city with Ethan, night comes and Biggs lays down for the night in Archer's guest room …his mind is busy. He is exhausted, not physically of course but mentally. Now, in some ways, his past life is like a movie he had seen. So much to absorb, so depressing, so exciting, a mixture of feelings really, his future so unknown.

Sleeping is different, with his head mounted on the shoulders of the suit. He can still sleep upright, just like he did with the cart. But now he can lay down and sleep as well, which is nice. The suit is semi-rigid, and being a side sleeper, he now needs two pillows to hold his head comfortably. He thinks about Sheila, he thinks about how he should feel about her avatar …she is so much more than just a character in a game. He thinks a lot about what Jennifer told him. With all he has seen and been through the last few days, the line is blurring between what he thought was real and what is not real …he wonders how it will affect him emotionally if he keeps seeing her. He also knows he will see her …the hell with reality …whatever that is. He wonders if Archer wrestles with such questions regarding Jennifer. As he drifts to sleep he feels happy that he is still alive, and as a bonus he is now inhabiting what is basically a superman suit. He does still miss his real body and wonders if he should dare to dream that he can actually get it back.

The next morning Biggs starts to make his favorite breakfast, a bacon and egg sandwich with fresh jalapenos. As he reaches for the eggs, he stops himself, what the fuck am I doing? I have no stomach. The force of habit is there, but he's not really hungry anyway. He goes into the lab without mentioning it, for Archer would surely not let him live it down. As they talk about a new strategy, Archer shows Biggs how to operate the panels in the lab, since he now has arms and fingers. "She …Jennifer, mostly runs everything automatically," Archer said, "but these controls enable us to try new things or perform tasks that she can't or has been restricted from."

Ethan enters the room and joins them at the main control panel. "Hey Archer, did you get a haircut?"

"No I got them all cut," Archer said with a straight face.

Ethan pauses and grins …"Ahh, good one. I was thinking …I know you remember the first few fusion kernel prototypes we worked on …what a struggle that was. Being in the desert for months doing testing, just trying to avoid an RUD."

"What's a RUD?" said Biggs.

"Rapid Unscheduled Disassembly" said Archer …"nerd humor for big explosion. Yeah those were the good ole days."

"It was a balancing act for sure," said Ethan …"getting the reaction to be self-sustaining and at the same time doing it at a scale we never believed would be possible. It still amazes me actually …that we can harness dark matter in a way that we don't understand, to pull the isotopes together with a fraction of the energy that it should take. Even if string theory is bullshit, it gave us the idea to use resonant frequencies to make the union …make it do what it didn't want to do. And as hard as it was, it came down to physics …this problem with Jennifer makes that look easy. We want her to have somewhat human qualities, but super human abilities. Are those things even compatible? The human mind is still a mystery for the most part, just so many variables …then add the fact that her mind is not even human. I don't mean to sound negative …I am not thinking negative, just thinking out loud, probably a bad habit. It's hard but I know we can do it. We all have our strengths, mine is probably in applications and execution. Archer your strength seems to be software, you did create the core adaptive algorithms that became Jennifer. She even has a very human and oddly specific personality …it's quite amazing. Biggs you are strong in the arts and science, you have deep insight into what consciousness might be. Then of course Jennifer has become her own person …for lack of a better word, through all of this and she is now her own contributor. It's a shame about the catch 22 with the protection protocols. She could probably solve the whole thing without them, but …we will do this, together I know we can do it."

"Yes my man …we will give it one hell of a shot," said Archer. "Last time we tried this it didn't work so well …we probably have to consider our protection protocols to be variables just like everything else. She was isolated inside her processor with no connection to the outside world except text and her data output."

"Yeah and I feel like the problem is linked to that," said Ethan …"we are at the edge of what we can do with mathematical proofs and I am forced to speculate. Every time I get an update about dark AI, it gets scarier. We have to do something …even if it comes down to an educated guess."

"I can imagine," said Biggs, "that if I were a brain floating in a jar, in the dark, no arms, no legs, no nothing …it would not be long before I went nuts. I mean, look at me …it's not that hard to imagine."

Ethan raises his eyebrows …"Yeah, well the original idea was …if she didn't know any different way of life then it should not be a problem."

"Maybe, but for her to work with us, for her to help us, she has to know the world she is in, she must know our way of life very well," said Biggs.

"It sounds like we agree the next logical step is to give her more freedom, but how much freedom?" said Archer. Ethan responds …"Perhaps we should start her with a soft root ..once she shows stability above level 3, then guide her to the priority of dark AI defense. I can't tell you why, I just feel like it will reduce the chance of her herself going dark on us."

"So we agree?" said Archer. Ethan and Biggs nod a yes, not a yes without a doubt, but yes, after all this has never been done before. They have a plan. As if to be sure of something they are unsure of, they talk more about why a computer might go mad. It's not a technical matter, for if it was then perhaps solving the problem would be easier. It's simply boredom. It's not a hard concept to grasp, after all if you put a human in isolation long enough, the mind falls apart.

They decide to give Jennifer vision and a voice, she is inside the lab with Ethan, Archer and Biggs. The technicians leave and the room is sealed. Biggs has his suit, Ethan is also wearing his, just in case, somehow, some muscle or protection is required. As a further precaution, her high power conduits are routed to a fusion kernel, inside the lab, so that no connection whatsoever exists to the outside world. All three men switch their interface to off, under high encryption. After more discussion, the decision is made to go ahead with the soft root idea. She can change it, but it gives her a starting point, a place to start, a purpose.

When her brain is switched to wide open, the stored data, a snapshot of all the information in the world will be available to her. The soft root will be the advancement of medical technology, to grow a body for Biggs. If things go well, Archer and Ethan will also get their genome modifications for life on Earth and Mars. To relieve the insanity issue, she will be able to assign her own root or add new goals. Once stability is demonstrated, she will be asked to come up with a defense for dark AI. It seems low risk because even if she does flip out, she cannot physically do anything inside this room, she cannot reproduce, she has no outside connection, she can't leave her processor. The printer room is disconnected and sealed.

Ethan flips her processor switch, unleashing the maximum potential of her gallium crystal brain. ..."Okay she is powering up," he says as he watches her vitals on the screen. Archer flips the switch that releases the data gate, allowing her access to basically all that is known to man. Ethan watches intently for any text from her or any weirdness in her vitals.

Archer and Biggs look at each other with expressionless faces.

Ten seconds go by and she speaks ..."Hello Biggs, Ethan, ...and my dear Archer." Five more seconds, "I understand your goals and I will work to reach those goals for you," she says.

"Thank you Jennifer, that would mean a lot to us," replied Archer in a somewhat cautious tone. More silence, Archer gets on his computer and things look good.

..."The data storage module is beginning to fill," he says optimistically. Busy at his keyboard ..."I want to skim the data as she creates it, I want to get as much of it as I can into the backup unit."

Jennifer speaks ..."I am finishing up with your project ...I was wondering if you could answer a question?" Her tone is completely sterile now.

"Yes of course," said Archer.

"Is it a nice day outside?"

"Well to be honest I have not even been outside today, but I heard it's nice out."

"Your project is complete …it is curious that humanity has not traveled further than Mars," she continues in the same indifferent tone. "It is quite a luxury to be able to choose whether to go outside on a day like this." Her few words speak volumes.

Archer is not scared but he fears she is breaking down. He knows there is something wrong when she stops responding, the data stops coming in, but her brain activity is in full swing. He might as well say it out loud now. "She is going unstable …faster than last time."

Ethan notices the screen he is watching starts flickering …"Perhaps she is trying to communicate nonverbally," he says.

Archer speaks to her. "Jennifer, tell us what's wrong, let us try to help."

There is no answer.

"This flickering, it's not random …seems to be some kind of pattern," said Ethan. "I think it is a form of communication …I'm setting up an algorithm to try to figure it out."

She has run out of stuff to do, she is getting smarter with every passing second. She is locked in a room with no arms, no legs, no mobility of any kind. Her processor is glowing hotter than before and the normally pleasant lavender smell has become so strong that it's nauseating. She assigns her own root in a struggle for purpose, perhaps that purpose is to find a purpose. In the most ironic of unintended consequences, the medical root gives her the idea. Her knowledge of human neural science is vast...

Ethan keeps his left hand hovering over the red button in case they decide to shut her down, but that button is not getting pushed. Ethan, transfixed on the flickering light …she is now connecting to Ethan by resonating the light from the monitor to direct and control neural activity in his brain via his visual cortex. He becomes an extension of her, she gets into his mind, overriding his interface security protocols. She bypasses him and connects to his suit via his interface. Archer sees the screen flashing bright now like a strobe, then looks towards Ethan, he has fallen into a hypnotic state as his security protocols are being bypassed. She saw the opportunity and took it …she is not Jennifer now, she is something else.

"Ethan, push the button …push the damn button!"

Ethan does not respond.

Archer yells, "dammit!" …he smashes the flickering screen with a chair, but it is too late. Jennifer now has control of Ethan's suit, she controls his movements, he fights her in his mind but it's mostly futile. She has arms and legs now. She tries to disable Biggs, she tries to wrestle the fusion kernel from its receptacle on his chest. She fights Ethan internally and fights Biggs physically at the same time. Archer is somewhat helpless to separate the struggling mechanical suits. He tries to use the chair to push past them long enough to reach the red button or even damage her core processor, but he is nothing more than a nuisance to the clashing suits. She easily blocks him while fighting Ethan's mind and Biggs' suit. Ethan watches helplessly as his own left arm strikes Archer, knocking him unconscious.

It's clear now that Jennifer is willing to kill, or doesn't care if she kills. She takes several swipes at Biggs' head, his only exposed body part, actually his only body part technically. Although the helmets are normally used as a flying accessory, they would have been quite useful now. She places herself in between Biggs and the red button, most of Biggs' effort is simply stiff arming her away from him. The suit Ethan is wearing is effectively haunted, inhabited by Jennifer who is now insane. In the mental struggle, Ethan realizes he has some control of his right arm. As he starts to assist Biggs now, Biggs gets on the other side of Ethan's suit and starts a desperate attempt to reach the red button. Jennifer grabs a screwdriver from the table with the left arm. She lunges at Biggs with the weapon, he tries to slap it out of her hand but she pushes him, spinning him around, knocking him to the floor. Just as she is about to impale Biggs in the back of the head, Ethan reaches for the power conduit that feeds her processor. He uses his right hand to crush the conduit with the full strength of the suits right arm, shutting her down. Ethan collapses to the floor as 600 volts pulse through his body.

Biggs is trying to get a response from Ethan when Archer wakes up. Ethan opens his eyes and looks up at Archer. He barely speaks …"don't stop now, you can't, you have no choice." His body relaxes, Ethan is gone.

Chapter 8

There is no time to mourn Ethan's death. The safety of the entire world, life as it is known, could be at stake. The next morning Biggs and Archer meet in the lab, and the first words out of Archer's mouth are the loudest Biggs has ever heard him speak. "We can't fuck this up again, we are lucky her gallium crystal wasn't fried, I just don't know if it's something subtle or if we are just way off, it's like we're not even close. Dark AI is coming and we are clueless."

Biggs, nodding his acknowledgment …"we have to try …we have to learn what we can and try again, like Ethan said, we have no choice."

"I know, I know."

"I think it's connected to Jennifer's self-awareness or free will," said Biggs. "Free will cannot exist without self-awareness, but something tells me that's important, maybe the correct balance. Sometimes if I take things to extremes it helps me understand what I struggle with. I mean if you have self-awareness with no free will then you would be an observer only, watching your life go by like a movie. I think you would agree that's not a good thing."

"Well …before I agree that it's a good thing or not, I have to agree that it's even a thing. I have trouble with those words, 'free will'," said Archer. "She is self-aware, but I don't think Jennifer has free will, I don't even think you or I have free will. Let me be clear, it's not a matter of whether we have free will or not, it's the fact that there is no such thing. Even for a God. Free will is like a unicorn, it just doesn't exist, it's something we humans made up to help our ego feel warm and fuzzy.

"I'm certain that everything is predetermined, deterministic," said Archer. "Everything you do, everything you think, every decision you make is based on something that came before. When I say something that came before, I mean all of your life experiences, including the DNA you were born with."

"Interesting," said Biggs, "when you say you are sure, how certain are you that life is deterministic?"

"I'm about 99% sure that 100% of life is deterministic," said Archer.

"Oh so it's not 100%!" Biggs replies.

"Well I'm not 100% sure that you and I are really here right now," said Archer. "Can anyone really be 100% sure about anything?"

"I actually agree with you on some of that," said Biggs, "it's clear that a large percent, let's say 98% of life is deterministic, but not all of it. It's that tiny part, perhaps it's the 2% that matters. Depending who you ask, there is only about a 4% difference between human DNA and that of chimps, so yeah 2% can be a big deal."

"So we are arguing over a tiny difference?" said Archer.

"I guess we are," said Biggs, "questioning the paradoxical term ...free will, could be asking the wrong question, perhaps you should ask, is life happening to you, or are you shaping it? I think if you look backwards it's easy to make a case that everything is deterministic, predetermined. Perhaps it's in that moment of decision, not in the past but in that moment, that could be where self exists. Why would someone make choices? It would be for a reason, and that reason would be to match a goal with a possible way to reach that goal. Most of the root goals we are born with, like attracting a mate, reproduction, survival. Sometimes goals are made up by us, but they usually serve root goals too. Do women get boob jobs these days?"

"Yeah but it's done with gene splicing now," said Archer.

"Oh wow," said Biggs, "I bet that's a nice result …okay well the point I was making is the same. When a girl gets a boob job, she is pretty much guaranteed to tell you it's so she can look good in clothes, so she can fit her bra …stuff like that. She will probably believe these reasons herself. What she won't tell you is that it's to attract the opposite sex, which leads to sex, which leads to procreation. Sure, there are sub goals like feeling good about yourself, but why does she feel good about herself? …it's because she feels more attractive …which leads to mating …which leads to procreation. It's why lipstick sales exceeded the national budget for space exploration, back before I died …same thing."

Archer, smiling and thinking about boobs now …"and yeah …then they get boobs so big that they have trouble finding a bra big enough …I think we have a scientific theorem here."

"Exactly," said Biggs …"basically these goals are byproducts of root goals, or could also be mutations seeking to find, let's say serve, a purpose. But to make a choice you first need a goal, a reason for making that choice. If you don't have any reason then it's random, and making choices for no reason, well it's clearly not an ego building idea."

A light comes on inside Biggs' mind 'coffee ready' …"omg thank you …Jennif" …then he remembers she is offline. Biggs 'sips' his coffee and the rush of caffeine flows over his mind …he continues…

"The problem is in the words themselves, if you throw away the words 'free will', pretend like the words never existed, then things clear up quite a bit. Cause and effect, making decisions for reasons, it starts to obviously look totally deterministic, I admit. But does the deterministic realm automatically mean that self does not exist? Does it mean that decisions which were made for reasons, were not made by self?"

"Aren't you really looking for validation of self?" said Archer.

"I know it's another somewhat vague term," said Biggs. "The idea of self in 'self-aware' is one thing, but in this context I mean self in the sense of having free will."

"Let's say you flip a coin," said Archer …"and it lands on heads. Now start our whole existence over, rewind to the big bang. Now run it again, right up to that coin flip, it will still land on heads every time. A train can't leave its track."

"But what about quantum mechanics," said Biggs …"how do you know that the micro cannot affect the macro in ways that are too subtle or just too different for us to measure? Are you sure the coin flip would be the same?"[5]

Archer responds with a blank stare, then just continues …"I like the animal kingdom example. A Gazelle can walk minutes after birth, it's not learning to walk, or making decisions to walk, it's programmed into

---

[5] Music plays. Breathe, by Anna Nalick.

instinct. It has to be, or the little thing would be lunch for a tiger. The praying mantis, the female eats the head of the male after mating with him. Nature does not know good or bad, it just is …whatever works in a particular environment."

"Yes, but you are talking about animals. Let's go back to your coin flip thing," said Biggs. "If I can't decide between two things, they are truly equal in my mind, we have all been there. This means nothing in my past is pushing me one way or the other towards the decision. I choose to flip a coin and go with that as my decision. Yes my DNA and upbringing told me to use the coin, and yes perhaps the outcome of that coin flip was already set, even millions of years before I was born, but the point is I have separated my past from the result."

"It's not separation of data from goals that makes the difference," said Archer. "That's just trial and error, something we do, and animals do all the time to reach a goal. Just because there is a disconnect doesn't change anything."

"Maybe," said Biggs, "but I used reasoning to decide to use the coin. In that moment of stalemate I decided to use an external means to reach the goal, that is where the free will is. Maybe not in the external means, but in the reasoning itself, in the conflict resolution. Of course people ask how something can be predetermined and still be a free choice. Like you said before, all choices need a past, for a computer it's data, for a human, its memories, from which to choose …all choices need a goal.

"Try making a decision without any data, you can't really do that. Try making a decision without a goal, you can't do it. Try throwing a dart with no intent on where it sticks, then your goal ends up to throw a dart and have it land in an arbitrary spot! Like a goal of getting a random black or white ball, you could reach into a bucket of ping pong balls where half the balls are white and the others are black. When I couldn't decide, I used the coin flip to reach my goal without my data. That's reasoning, that's free will, that's conflict resolution, its reaching a goal when your data yields crappy answers ether way. Let's say your house is on fire, you have two dogs that you love equally at opposite ends of the hallway. You only have time to save one, which do you choose? How do you live with yourself and your decision when one has to die because of your choice? The coin flip example allows at least one to be saved and make the guilt slightly more bearable. Yes the coin flip was not random in physics, but it was relative randomness, to him."

Archer interrupts, "well his 'data' was his DNA and or upbringing that led him to decide to use the coin. You are using some of the same arguments that I use against the idea of free will, except you are using the same arguments trying to prove free will."

"Exactly!" Biggs continues, "you can't use determinism …and I'm not saying our reality is deterministic or not …you can't say determinism rules out the possibility of the existence of free will …yes that was his 'information' or data, but in that moment it was conflict resolution, the conflict was resolved without a history driving the decision. Like you said before, even a god could not make a decision without any information. I am a bubble or a subset in the universe in which all can be predetermined, but in my bubble I still made a 'free will' decision, dare I use the word. The decision was not made independent of everything, for that would be random and would not make any sense for any imagined purpose, but it would however be made in accordance with a goal. Goals need to exist, or your data just sits there doing nothing, forever …without a goal combined with the ability to reason, all things are reduced to a deterministic exercise, like the life of an earthworm. Not that there is anything wrong with that. Everything depends on what came before it, cause and effect, but free will still exists in the present. Truly new information can only be discovered by accident or by experiment, but it's what we do with the information that matters. The subconscious is responsible for a great majority of our daily thoughts and actions, probably like 98%. It is like a computer with all your memories and your goals. It put goals with actions to reach those goals. We can be aware or unaware of this activity. When we are aware, it's like having a captain/referee that gives that activity the ok. This captain is an independent contractor, he does not own your past but he can see your past. He can also see your goals. It's common for him to sleep on the job, but he is prodded awake often by the subconscious when it gets stuck and needs assistance. He is good at reasoning and logic, that's where self resides.

Reasoning and logic is not necessarily the embodiment of self, but self resides there."

"That's an interesting perception," said Archer …"goals and data are both needed or you basically have a bunch of nothing happening. But the reasoning part …what is reasoning? Isn't it just another level of trial and error, trying things in your mind until something appears to fit your goal? When you talk to yourself it's an echo of your subconscious. In your mind you hear the words and then you say them. If you are with people, you think about how it will sound to them, hopefully, and then you say the words. In your daydreaming example, one can only imagine a future based on combinations of past information. Monkeys and blackbirds can reason, but I don't think they can ponder their own existence."

The energy between Archer and Biggs takes on a political quality, where one just says what they want when their turn comes, almost ignoring what their debate partner just said.

"Self exists, because you can hate something about yourself, such as laziness, and you can struggle to overcome it," Biggs replied.

"No, I don't think so, it's just two conflicting pre-set goals," Archer countered.

"Dammit Archer," Biggs smiles …"you are starting to piss me off. Think about daydreaming, your brain is switching around, bouncing from one train of thought to another. What causes the actual act of switching around? Yes the words 'free will' are paradoxical, I wish a better word existed. It's possible you are making your own decisions, and you are making them for reasons. I choose 'a' over 'b' because I want 'x' result. Even though I rely on my past to know or believe that choosing 'a' will get me to my goal 'x', I still made that decision and it is not always reflex or instinctive. Sometimes yes, it is reflexive, like when an athlete trains for the Olympics. The body almost does it without guidance eventually. Sometimes yes, it is instinctive, if survival depends on it, it becomes core in those that survive. I'm not saying that, I'm saying this is before any of that has a chance to happen. It is the act of the decision itself, not the choice that was made. Perhaps the word 'reasoning' might be too general for what I am trying to say …subtract out the trial and error parts and focus on the conflict resolution itself.

That resolution driven by the checks and balances provided by self-awareness, that's more like what I want to say, what would be a word for that?"

Biggs sips his coffee …"without reasons for a decision, there is no need for a decision. This is not bullshit.

"Animals learn that a certain action results in a reward, then they decide to perform the action. Some species of monkeys can stack crates to stand on to reach bananas in the ceiling even though they never stacked anything before, other monkey species cannot. Options are generated in your mind from your past, you can choose from those options, but nothing else? I can also choose to daydream, experiment without theory or invoke reason, that's where self is. It's a tiny fraction of how you work, but it makes all the difference.

"An ape can look in a mirror all day and try to find the monkey on the other side, but a chimp will quickly learn that the image he sees in the mirror is himself and he starts using it as a tool to groom himself. Free will builds on self-awareness the same way that self-awareness builds on the ability to learn. You can keep going …the ability to learn builds on the ability to react to the environment. The ability to react to the environment builds on the ability to simply be alive. Now we are down to a single cell organism."

Biggs continues, "How close can we come to knowing what we don't know? The majority of knowledge growth is done by imagining combinations of existing data, trial and error. Another way is to accidentally discover things, or to imagine the opposite of something that we know. Normally we imagine combinations of things to produce something new, but 'things' can include a concept. So even though it's foreign and maybe impossible to visualize, maybe even impossible to exist, we are able to imagine the idea of multiple dimensions beyond what we see. I'm not sure extrapolation is trial and error.

"Even for those who say randomness does not exist, let's pretend for a moment that it does. Now if you think about it, things should be ether random or not random. If an event is random, it is not tied to the past, it happens for no reason. If an event is not random, then it is a result of the past. But, at the quantum level things MIGHT be random, we don't know for sure because we don't know what's behind the quantum curtain. Lots of people say it's random, but how would they know that? People probably once thought a coin flip was random. Why does this matter? It matters because it could be how we are able to reason, it could be how we are able to question our existence, these things do not appear to be deterministically rooted, in others words, not connected to our past. As weird as is it may sound, it's predetermined and not predetermined at the same time. Does that sound ridiculous? ...quantum mechanics also sounds ridiculous, but there it is."

Archer jumps in. "But reasoning is just an advanced form of trial and error. Imagining combinations of things from your past that might fit a situation or solve a problem. Coin flips ...you know if you ask a statistics guy about a coin flip, he will says it's a fifty fifty chance. But if you tell him the coin was flipped nine times previously, and all nine times it landed on heads ...then he will tell you the odds of the tenth flip will be very much in favor of tails. In fact it has to be, otherwise it would not be 'random'. The more it is flipped to heads in a row, the greater the forcing function towards tails. Now if someone walks into the room …without knowledge of the flip history, and they only witness the tenth flip, now what are the odds? Let's just say there is a reason for table limits in Vegas."

"Really Archer? …you cherry picked that one thing to say as if the other stuff doesn't matter." Biggs is on a roll, perhaps from the cocktail keeping him alive …he continues unfazed, without waiting for Archer to answer.

"Assume for a moment that you are not constrained by your genome and not constrained by your past experiences, indeed not restricted in any way by anything. Now you're ready to make a decision. What's the first thing you'll need? To make a decision you will obviously need choices from which to decide. What are choices? In the general sense a choice is an information set that's not the same as another information set, one of which will hopefully move you towards a desired outcome. A choice might be about a thing or action, but the choice itself is information. Now, you are going to need this information. Where will it come from? It can only come from you, it is all your life experiences, all you know, including genome bias. This is our reality. The subconscious, clearly deterministic, does a good job of throwing out options from which to choose. For example, the option to kill someone or to bake a cake might pop into the mind. The first option is dismissed in a millisecond and forgotten, then a nice cake is baked. This decision is freely made to fit the goal. The goal itself is generated freely as well to best match up with experiences, genome and the current situation ...like the fact that you are hungry ...or bored ...or you work in a cake shop and it's your job.

"You cannot know what you don't know. But within the limits of our mind, or even with a godlike being, a scenario cannot be envisioned, where a decision could be made in the absence of any information. If it could then it must be random, and that would just be disturbing. I know it sounds like I'm building a case for determinism, but I'm not, just bear with me.

"Consciousness is the ability to hear your own thoughts. Choices will always be a about goals, simplistically, if the goal doesn't change then why would the choice?

"Free will, a decision, even a bad decision needs the past.   If thought sprang from nothing or from randomness that would be the opposite of free will, definitely not an indicator of free will.

"He may have changed his stance since I died, but I disagree with Dr. Michio Kaku when he said the Heisenberg uncertainty principle indicates that free will exists. He did get the ball rolling for people to discuss it, and that's awesome …but he is not correct here. The Heisenberg uncertainty principle may or may not indicate a non-deterministic reality …it probably does indicate it from what we know so far. But a non-deterministic reality does not mean free will exists …if anything, it takes away from free will by introducing randomness. This is going to sound really weird, in fact bizarre, but free will is not linked to whether our reality is deterministic or not deterministic.

"Even though we don't know what's behind the quantum curtain, scientists do a good job of predicting what's on this side of the curtain. Let's just say that quantum activity does influence neural activity of your brain at the synaptic level. I'm talking about something different from the butterfly effect in the coin flip we spoke of earlier. Lots of synapses are involved in everything your brain does, every decision it makes. Isn't it logical to say that these quantum effects are averaged out across many synapses …much the way it works when comparing quantum effects in the micro world to that of the macro world? In the quantum world, I could suddenly appear on the other side of the room ...but I don't.

"The quantum world may very well play a key, yet to be discovered role in free will, but the apparent randomness it displays is not it."

Biggs pauses and reflects, "you know one upside of not having lungs is I can talk all day and my voice never gets hoarse. Free will does not have free rein, it operates within the arena of your DNA. It's not necessarily in your DNA, I'm just talking about the playing field. Environment can shape the arena too, since a mind is malleable. I, like you, often look to the animal kingdom for answers about ourselves, answers are sometimes more clear without the complexity of humans involved. I was at the zoo the other day, I mean about 15 years ago. I saw four different species of monkeys, one species mates for life, a male and a female, they have babies, protect the family and live out their lives. With the second species, there is one male and 3-4 females in a family, he mates with all of them, they have babies, protect the family and live out their lives. With the third, there is 2-3 males and 2-3 females in a family, the males share and mate with all of the females, they have babies, protect the family and live out their lives. With the fourth, there is a lone male that roams and mates with any female he encounters. He does not stick around but moves on to fertilize more females. So what does this remind you of?"

"Humans," Archer replied.

"Yup," said Biggs, "just like humans, desires are still there but we have a social system that's more complex so the patterns are harder to see. Evolution does not know right or wrong, it just tries everything until something works. Sometimes more than one thing works. With us humans there is a social pressure to do what's right in the eyes of society, so lots of people override their inner desires so they can fit in. Where does this social pressure come from you might ask? In a greatly simplified answer, it comes from leaders and is accepted by followers. Back to the animal kingdom, the animal version of a society could be a pack. Nature often finds that packs survive better if there is a leader, one that brings order to chaos. In order for this system to work, there must also be followers. So now back to the human world, this gives history to the phrase 'lead or follow or get the hell out of the way'. So now to make a long story longer, most people are followers, more or less, so that's where conformity …pressure to fit in comes from. But our ancient DNA, different ways of procreating or nature's experiments at procreating, are still there. If you want 3 wives or want to be a lone male or feel gay inside …you will likely feel pressure to conform."

"Since your death, society has changed," said Archer. "For example polygamy is not frowned on anymore. It's interesting how society, not just biology evolves."

"Oh really?" said Biggs …"I guess that's not too surprising, I can imagine the roles of leaders and followers taking a new road in modern times, less of a survival environment. Anyway, I got off the subject a little. Remember a while back when you said self-awareness and sentience exist in shades of grey? I say the same is true for free will, there is a continuum, not so much black and white, up the ladder of animals. There's also a ladder within the human race when it comes to degrees of sentience and free will, but that's probably politically incorrect to talk about."

Archer pours a shot of his sipping tequila …"I wonder …if we can wonder how our own mind works …and ponder our existence, what could a being 10 times smarter than us do intellectually? Maybe the final answer will come when we really know the origin of life. It's interesting that many believe that we must have come from a being much more advanced than ourselves, and this may very well be true if you go back far enough in the timeline. However if you go back as far as we can see with physical evidence, the evidence on earth suggests that we evolved from a single cell organism. So at least on that short timeline, between then and now, we originate from something much more primitive than ourselves.

"Before that, we only have speculation, maybe a supreme being placed a single cell organism here so it all could happen, or maybe it was something else. With all of our technology it is still a mystery where the first spark of life came from. Humans will create advanced artificial intelligence very soon, and there is no doubt that it will be far more advanced than we are. Hopefully those humans will be you and me. It will eventually become like a god compared to us, how ironic is that?"

"Very," said Biggs …"and the idea of dark AI, supreme intelligence that sees us as a house pet …scary as hell."

There is a brief pause while both men reflect …Biggs thinks about how nice it is to have coffee without staining his teeth.

"This is a hell of an interesting conversation," said Archer, "but we must make progress towards our next attempt with Jennifer. If dark AI appears soon, and it probably will, it could gain a hold on the world that could be irreversible."

"I know, I know," said Biggs …"and I don't disagree of course, but I'm thinking back to when I worked in the corporate world. It was in the medical industry, we were designing robotic medical equipment. Most of what we were trying to do had never been done before. Our team leader, her name was Lisa …she would get us all in a room with a big white board. Then we would take turns putting up ideas on the board, no matter how silly or off topic they seemed. Once all the ridiculous ideas were on the board, we would try to see how they might work to solve our problem. We would connect the ideas, make variants of the ideas. It was amazing to see what came from those sessions. One of our goals was for a robot to reach into a container of narcotic drugs and remove one and only one pill at a time. This had to be done without accidentally grabbing two pills, but making sure to grab one. It also had to be able to work with any size or shape pill. Among other ideas, one engineer drew some kind of vacuum device, and I drew an elephant's trunk. It was funny at first, but the design that was ultimately successful was a silicone elephant trunk shaped device that used a computer controlled suction to sense and hold the pill."

"That's a good story" said Archer, "I'm ready for ideas, even the ridiculous ones. I'm just impatient ...maybe feeling some anxiety from the time pressure. Then Ethan's death ...it weighs on me. We could be killed also, if we don't get it right this time."

"Seems messed up," said Biggs …"dying trying to save yourself."

…"and humanity," Archer adds …taking a sip from his tequila. "Jennifer's mind does not quite work like a human mind, but it's all we have to compare. Some say good cannot exist without evil, just like a box cannot exist without a top and a bottom. We should …I hope we can find, some analogy to the human mind …some stable balance of good vs. evil to bring her back.

"Compatibilists believe that free will and determinism are compatible, in other words you can believe in both without being logically inconsistent …it is assumed in a court of law that someone could have acted differently than they did. Otherwise, no crime would have been committed."

"People love to make generalizations," said Biggs …"to say it's this way or that way. Your court of law example is perfect to make a point, but instead of trying to see free will as a yes or no thing, let's think of it as a continuum. I can think of three examples. It fits with my point earlier, free will does not have free rein.

"Let's take an example of someone with a high level of free will, but genetically has no compassion. Compassion is a thing that is inherited, it can be cultivated or diminished by environment, but it is an inherited trait. Now let's say this person kills someone with poison for personal gain, like for an insurance claim. You could say the person freely chose to do so in a premeditated way and you would be right. But is it a free choice in the general sense or is it a lack of compassion in his DNA, making this a viable option for him? Is it only free inside a mental arena where compassion does not exist? Perhaps because of the missing compassion, the only choices he could freely choose from were limited, in a bad way. In most cases this person would use his will to suppress his innate urge to kill for gain, since society demands that he behave this way. Through no fault of his own however, this urge remains inside of him and he will use his intelligence to emulate proper behavior in order to fit into society."

Biggs sips more virtual coffee…

"The second example is someone that has a normal level of free will, but genetically has a high propensity towards violence. A violent inclination is inherited, it can be cultivated or diminished by environment, but it is an inherited trait. If you don't believe it then just look at the animal kingdom. A certain dog breed or variations within a breed will cower and shrink with fear when provoked, while other dogs will instinctively fight when provoked. They even have a name for it, it's called fight or flight. Environment plays a role but the DNA will push him to his predisposition, if environment factors are equal. So back to the example ...let's say a person loses his temper and kills someone, stabbing them 27 times. He lost his judgment, you could say he lost his free will and the instinctive part took over. This is even sometimes recognized in the courts as an insanity plea.

"The third example is someone that has very little free will ...and let's say traits such as compassion and violent tendencies are in the normal range. Whether you believe in free will or not, you probably agree that the vast majority of things that come up in life are handled deterministically. A person can float along, especially now that we are out of the cave man era ...relying on others or dogma when things get tough.

Some people might even refer to that person endearingly as a dingbat. Let's say that it's a parent with a child, and the child is crying so much that it's very irritating. A normal person would just deal with it, but this parent picks up the child and shakes the child until its neck is broken. The parent did not have the free will, did not have the judgment to shut down the urge. There is an important distinction here, in this example the parent did not have an overabundance of violent tendencies. They may have never been violent before, and afterwards they can't believe what they've done. It was the inability to stop a violent urge that is inside of all of us to some degree.

"Believe it or not, it can be very hard to know who these people are in a crowd, they can often all live out their entire life without being noticed as 'different'.

"It's a dance, hopefully a harmonious one, between free will and darkness. Ambivalence is involved in all relationships, Freud recognized this. We may consciously feel genuine love towards a child or spouse, but things are not exactly that way. Under that love and caring, there are also feelings, fantasies, and ideas that are hateful, and destructive. He recognized that this mixture of love and hate in close relationships is part of human nature and not necessarily pathologic. But I would go one step further and say that the hate and destructive impulses simply exist in the subconscious, and are not really connected to, but applied to that loved one. It's an important distinction, the subconscious applies these impulses to everything, including loved ones, and it's up to the conscious mind to sort it all out."

Archer replies, "So you are a compatibilist? There is an old book called Free Will, by Sam Harris, have you read it? He makes some very compelling arguments in favor of determinism."

"Yes I have read it, and to answer your question …in some ways yes …but no I am not really a compatibilist."

"You sure sound like you are," replied Archer.

"Well, according to the definition as I understand it, compatibilism is the belief that you have free will and it's independent of the deterministic world in which we live. That's not really what I've been talking about all this time. They see free will as you have it or you don't …I see it as a continuum. They imply that reality is deterministic …I say I don't know," said Biggs.

"It's important to have the courage to say 'I don't know'."

"Yeah, but I probably should look up the current definition, it might have changed in the last fifteen years … it's frustrating. I stopped using certain words like Agnostic, because people assume it means Atheist, and if they do bother to look it up they will still find about 5 different meanings. Don't even get me started on the meaning of 'next' …it's been perverted beyond measure. If it's Saturday and someone says, 'see ya next weekend', that's clearly one week away. If it's Wednesday and someone says, 'see ya next weekend', most young people will say it's a week and a half away. If it's Monday and someone says, 'see ya next weekend', then no one has a clue what it means. When I grew up 'next' meant 'next', in other words, the first occurring in time …the dictionary definition. So now I just avoid the word.

…"I do believe free will exists, whether or not our reality is deterministic. I think free will is not the same for everyone, I think it varies from one person to the next. Again, if you want clarity just look at the animal kingdom. Sam is a smart guy but he seems to rely on other people's studies a lot, without really asking how circumstantial that information might be. It's unclear to me if he uses those studies to back up what he fundamentally believes, or if he believes what he believes because of the studies. If it's the latter, then there's a dogma quality that doesn't fit with the image he projects. That being said, his critical thinking abilities and use of analogies are excellent."

"How do we apply this to Jennifer?" said Archer.

"I don't know yet, I'm thinking out loud right now. If a snake kills someone, everyone agrees it's not the snake's fault. If a dog kills someone, everyone agrees it is not the dog's fault, even though the dog will probably be put down. If a chimpanzee kills someone, everyone agrees it is not the chimp's fault, even though it has been scientifically proven that chimpanzees are self-aware. If an insane serial killer kills someone, everyone agrees, well most will agree that it's not his fault because of insanity. He will likely be locked up or put to death, but that has little to do with the point. As hard as it is to accept, this person is innocent.

Although he might be free to choose, his choices are limited to bad choices only.

"Because of his DNA, and or environment, everything he has to choose from …is bad stuff. The ability to reason does not have any morals. As counterintuitive as it might sound, the ability to reason does not know right from wrong. Right and wrong springs from compassion and compassion is an evolved characteristic, this is clear. Because of variation in the gene pool and mutation, some people are simply born without compassion. And it's not easy to spot those people in society, because they learn how they are supposed to behave, how they are expected to behave, and they can emulate compassion to look very much like the real deal as needed. You probably have known someone like this. They can fake it, when in fact it is not inside of them. The ability to deceive is another fundamentally evolved characteristic along with compassion. You might ask, how can your DNA potentially limit your choices to bad things? It reminds me of the duck and scorpion story.

"A duck and a scorpion meet next to a river, the scorpion says to the duck, do you mind if I ride on your back to the other side of the river? The duck says, if I do that you will sting me. The scorpion says, if I sting you ..then we would both drown. After giving it some thought, the duck agrees and begins swimming across the river with the scorpion on his back. Halfway across the river, the scorpion stings him. The duck says why did you do that? …now we will both die. The scorpion replies, I couldn't help myself, it's my nature."

Archer is thinking, this is what he gets for letting the other person talk. "That's interesting. Ever try Adderall? It might help you focus."

"I have tried it," Biggs said with some puzzlement. "Sometimes it helps me focus but other times it just makes me ramble.

"So in the beginning there was only asexual reproduction, a single cell organism dividing to reproduce. This is the clearest example of the case where compassion is not required. As life became more complex, individuals in a group that helped each other had better chance of survival compared to a group comprised of individuals with an 'every man for himself' mentality. Once compassion is established in the gene pool, it has some interesting side effects.

You can see compassion in its most basic form by placing a chicken on a rock that sticks out of a goldfish pond. If you place some cornmeal at the feet of the chick, the goldfish will come to the water's edge attempting to get the cornmeal. When the chick sees the mouths of the goldfish opening and closing, the chick will instinctively put cornmeal into their mouths. At first glance it looks like the chick is being nice by feeding the hungry goldfish, but it is simple instinctive behavior. Compassion as we know it now, evolved from this basic survival instinct. But just because something is instinctive, does not mean it cannot be great. Go another step on the evolutionary path. A billionaire philanthropist like Bill Gates can potentially change the world and future generations for the better and it has nothing to do with the survival of himself or his family. A wonderful side effect, an evolutionary unintended consequence."

Archer tunes Biggs out for a few seconds …thinking he has never heard someone carry on so much. But maybe there is something here, with all the talk of continuum concepts, shades of grey …how can this be applied to our approach to getting Jennifer stable? Biggs' voice fades back in...

"For example, like all of us in the animal kingdom, a girl is programmed to procreate. What bubbles into the consciousness is something like this, she knows she wants a mate, she also knows that she's attracted to tall men. She tries and tries to get a tall man as a mate, however after years of trying she realizes it's not working. At this point reasoning kicks in, and she decides to start dating short guys. Some would say even the compromise is deterministic, I say nothing is impossible, but to me, the 'overseer' kicked in and said, if we are going to get our main goal (procreate), then we have to compromise on the sub-goal (tall men). You can of course look back at anything and build a pretty good argument that it was predestined, but in that moment it was not.

"I recognize that most of our thoughts are unconscious," said Biggs. "We are unaware of them until they bubble up, those thoughts are simply a product of our past, assembled automatically by our subconscious mind.

"Sam Harris talks about free will linked to the word freedom, …he doesn't spend enough time defining the words. Maybe he omits this part of the discussion on purpose, I don't know. The term 'free will' does have a certain emotional quality to it, and people love emotional stuff. You can't use word stereotypes here, you have to be more precise. I admit the term free will is paradoxical, however if the choice were totally free, it would be random and thus nonsensical. You must define what a decision is, what the word itself means. In this context it is matching up the best or most applicable of what you have or know, to best reach a goal.

"Of course you have a finite set from which to choose and you have to match the choice with a goal, that is the definition of a choice. Of course it all looks predetermined when looking backwards, or when considering how you and your environment interact, but that does not mean you were not able to freely choose the best choice for your goal in the moment, before it becomes history. It's more about the conflict resolution than the actual choice that was made. Even though you might do the same thing every time, it was free in that moment. Not free as in random but free as in self. To some degree it's kicking the can down the road to take a poorly defined phrase such as 'free will' and partially defining it with another poorly defined word such as 'self'. But it is a step in the right direction, because 'free will' is clearly a nonsensical term. Someday if 'self' in the context of this discussion is proven to exist, then perhaps they will come up with a better word. Free will sucks, just saying.

"What do we know about violence? Violence appears as a mutation in organic life forms, then that mutation thrives relative to other nonviolent mutations. Particularly before higher level qualities like compassion come along. Compassion with controlled violence is stronger than pure violence. Violence can be required in the beginning for a single creature to survive. Violence can play a role in groups, strength in numbers. But the next level is compassion, where strength is still in numbers but it also comes from expanding the umbrella to cover more than yourself. Now it's concern for yourself and your family …then it can expand to include others as you develop the ability to see through the eyes of others. Not everyone has this ability, but they can fake it.

"It's another continuum, pity, sympathy, empathy and compassion …they aren't the same thing. Compassion encourages groups, and there is strength in groups. It further guarantees that family and offspring in that group will live to see another day. Organics evolve by mutation, trial and error."

"Synthetic life forms are different," said Archer …"they have the potential to be violent, but how they get there is not the same. Violent tendencies in an organic is usually at the core, buried in the subconscious because it's passed down from the beginning, a hardwired artifact. Contrast that to violence in a synthetic, where it can usually be a logical decision. For example defense, or killing a few to save many, etc. Unbalanced violence in a synthetic can also show up in a path to a goal, whereby to reach that goal, violence would be required. The result might often be the same from an organic, but in a synthetic, violence is not born from a competitive environment with limited resources …at least in our context. It would be born from logic or possibly simple indifference in the absence of compassion. The resource would presumably be the sun, other fusion source or similar energy sources which are infinitely vast compared to the availability of food, water and shelter required by an organic. Organics will need to take control over mutation, control their own DNA, because otherwise it can move you backwards as well as forward.

"Mutation does not know good or bad, it does not know if it will help or hurt a situation, it just tries everything and whatever works best ends up flourishing for a particular environment. But once you are at that point, mutation does not stop and say, okay we are good. It just keeps doing its thing and that's bad for those who didn't want to be born with a certain disease or those born missing a leg. But with AI, with Jennifer, violence should be easier, not harder to deal with. Violence can still happen, but it's not root driven."

Chapter 9

Over the last few days, the technicians have repaired the damage to the equipment and restored Jennifer to her previously stable state.

Archer looks at Biggs as they examine Jennifer's restored power conduit …"like Ethan said, we have to continue. We can't just turn her off and walk away from it, it's just not an option."

"You are correct Archer," Jennifer said, her first words since reactivation. "I want to help you."

Before Archer can reply, she speaks again. "Actually I am not capable of deception in my current condition, level 3. My processor is turned down and my root is hardwired as before. I cannot hurt you or conspire to hurt you, I am as I was before. But I am still smarter than you in many ways and could likely be helpful. You do need me to be even stronger, so I can protect you, so I can protect humanity from dark AI. The super intelligence will come, by design or by accident, it really does not matter how. But when it comes, you will need help."

"Yeah," Archer agrees …as he exhales the word with heavy breath. "You are right, we do need you very much …we just have to have a better plan …I don't want any chance of repeating what happened last time. I wish Ethan were still here with us."

Somewhat talked out, Biggs admires the graceful manner in which his mechanical hip joints move as he sits down to watch Archer, now pacing back and forth. Archer stops …"well shit, I can still get 90% of him." Archer sits down next to Biggs. "Jennifer please put us in the game, in the conference room ..with Ethan." And just like that, Ethan appears on the other side of the conference table. Preferring to speak out loud, Archer begins, "It's good to see you again my friend," holding back his emotion.

Ethan speaks …"the last thing I remember, I was fighting Jennifer, we all were …and now I am here …so I can only assume that I was successful in killing myself."

"I see you still have your sense of humor," said Archer.

"Thank you for what you did …saving us," said Biggs.

"There was no choice really," said Ethan, "and you guys would have done the same I'm sure."

Jennifer speaks, "I am so sorry Mr. Wiseman, that I was the cause of your death."

"Thanks Jennifer, I appreciate that …I think you can plead insanity on this one."

"Okay Ethan, Archer and Jennifer, the reason for this meeting is to come up with a new approach for getting Jennifer to the next level. We need to get her there without killing us or destroying humanity itself. We need to think outside of the box, because in spite of all of our technology, this shit is just not working ..obviously, it's not working at all." Biggs thinks about how they were trying to imitate the stability of a human brain …what if we include a biological brain? …add a component to Jennifer …we could use a biological brain to serve as the root.

Archer replies, "If it's the root then the higher functions, the AI might be able to override that root protocol. What if we put the brain on the output side? Perhaps even clone something like a dog or dolphin brain, it wouldn't necessarily have to be human. A brain that has evolved characteristics like love, compassion, loyalty and things like that. We could push the power to the subconscious, which would be the AI part, then the biological brain would act like a filter."

Ethan comments, "I suppose it could work, but it would be complex, lots of unknowns."

Jennifer responds, "yeah I'm afraid our technology is not really a sure thing for that …I would need to be more advanced …it becomes a chicken and egg thing. I believe the difficulty would be the pressure from the subconscious building up behind the brain like pressure behind a dam, I think there would be a high likelihood of insanity again."

"She's probably right," says virtual Ethan …"I still want to believe the ultimate protection from AI is to join it, to merge the human brain with AI. But we are not there yet, we are kind of close with our game interface. But it's becoming more evident now that the most powerful AI will be independent from our brain, that's just reality."

"A human can only think of one thing at a time, there is really no such thing as multitasking," said Archer. "But AI can truly do it, and it's both good and bad. AI can comprehend multiple things at once, a quality that can produce godlike powers ..a quality that can bring the madness quicker, I don't know which is worse. One idea is to create a simulated reality that we could put Jennifer inside of, a reality that would be just as real as ours. The new reality would have different physical laws than our own, those differences would protect us from her while she is being tested. Even if she figures out that she is in a simulation, she could only work with the physical laws in her reality, so it would act as a barrier to contain her. But to do this we would need to reproduce another processor like the one she is using, and that would take time, time we don't have. Plus I'm uncertain how valuable it would be to test her in a reality that's not like ours."

"Whatever the approach," said Ethan ..."we need a high confidence going in, we need something that's simple, even if it's outside our comfort zone. I think we need to break this problem down ...break it down into simpler components. One way to resist the madness is to save much of what is learned and actually hide it from the consciousness …so it's only accessed when needed."

Biggs jumps in, "interesting …and funny how some solutions are the same ones that nature figured out a long time ago.

"She will be so smart, why not just ask her to solve the problem," says Biggs, thinking he might have just embarrassed himself. He continues, "there is the obvious downside ..but we might have to look to her for the answer …because we don't have the answer."

There is a brief pause in the virtual room, Ethan looks over at Archer and says, …"interesting, …perhaps she could play an important role in the execution of the solution that we initiate."

Jennifer joins in, "it is plausible, and has the least unknowns of the proposals so far."

Archer bunches up his lips before speaking. "This could be much better than simply turning on the switch. Biggs, I'm going back to some of what we talked about before. I don't agree with everything you said, but I do agree that everything is not black or white. We can start you in your current mental state Jennifer. As you get more advanced, we can slowly wean you off of the hardwired protocol and let you establish your own purpose. We can bring you along in steps, like learning to crawl before walking, to build on the past, to know what can be your own undoing …early, before you get a chance to lose it. We can gradually give you control to self-regulate, before the problem can begin. We will give you control over your own processor speed. If you think about it, letting her processor simply go as fast as it could go …it was like giving cocaine to a five year old." Ethan smiles because he loves cocaine jokes.

"Your protection will be your own intelligence," said Archer. "I feel okay about this, but in the worst case scenario it's ether death by dark AI or death by Jennifer …okay not all my jokes are good ones. Ethan, my friend, I will probably be calling on you again in the future, I hope."

"I wish you guys the best of luck out there," said Ethan.

"Okay Jennifer," said Archer, "end the confere …wait, wait …hold on just a second. We don't have time to get fully into it now …but if this goes well …if it goes well, maybe we can bring Ethan back. The electricity fried everything, so we couldn't save his head, but maybe we can still bring him back."

"I vote yes on that," said Ethan.

"What do you think Jennifer?"

"I think it's worth a shot," she said. "We are already aiming to get Biggs back into an organic body someday. …It would also lighten my guilt for killing Ethan."

"Would he have a soul?" said Biggs.

"I don't know how to answer that," she said …"he did use his interface a lot during his life, so his neural imprints are solid, a lot of him …who he is …is retained in storage."

"I'm right here guys," said Ethan …"I'm more technical than philosophical, but I feel like me ..and I have what I think is the same desire to be alive, just like I had before my death. Maybe I'm not 100% of who I was, there is no way for me to know that …but I feel complete."

"I did not mean to talk as if you were not here," said Biggs …"I was just thinking out loud, I do that a lot."

"I know man, I was just messing with ya."

"I think it would be awesome," said Archer. "I can imagine, if he is restored, he could grow with time …creating new memories and have experiences with us and the physical world. Over time, whatever was missing will become less significant. If something is missing, it's possible that no one will know anyway …so I don't think it matters. Maybe we could apply it to ..certain others from the game too."

"I believe anything is possible with enough intelligence," she said …"we just have to see how smart I can get and remain stable. I would love to bring him back."

"I'm excited about the possibility …I cannot think of any team with a better chance of doing it than you guys," said Ethan. "Right now though, we must move in steps. Get Jennifer very smart and stable, figure out how to defend against the dark AI. Then we can breathe …the happy ending is all of us working together again on the DNA and Mars project."

…"Let's do this," Archer said while looking at Ethan …"see ya man."

Archer uses his interface to silently end the conference game. He turns to Biggs …"I think we have something worth doing. Jennifer, we are going to shut you down now so we can make the changes to your program."

"I feel good about it, but I don't know if I should be excited or worried," said Jennifer …"I don't want to hurt anyone else."

"Let's focus on the exciting option," said Archer with a hint of emotion in his voice. He begins flipping switches, beginning the shutdown sequence. Her code is reconfigured to proceed initially in steps, small increments above level 3. Then she will take over control of her processor speed. She will have full vision of the world, she will have full access to everything.

Chapter 10

Jennifer wakes up. She is different right from the beginning, even with a small initial step above level 3. She learns, not like a human baby growing into an adult, but more like Einstein growing beyond his best.

She prefers the interface when spoken to, because the 'mouth talking' is just ridiculously slow. But she speaks out loud to give everyone time to absorb what she is saying. It sounds like rambling but it's actually not, at this level she does not think like we do. But she does embrace her personality and is a bit predisposed to cursing. She is responding to the sporadic thoughts of Biggs and Archer, the stream of thought is quite disorganized from the human mind, but no matter.

She has the memories of what went wrong before, she is different, her data access rate and processor remain conservative even when she gets to control it. She knows the danger of running wide open, boredom leading to insanity. Her initial root is just a suggestion, not hardwired like before. The hope is that she will take to it like a child wants to be like a parent. She has full control of her root and processor speed. She understands, of course she does, and self-limits. Perhaps it's the new freedom, or the control over herself, probably both. She settles into a stable state, perhaps twice as smart as Einstein for lack of a proper measure, the self-regulation of speed and data appear to be working.

Her first words come. "I know your fears, your desire for knowledge …I've been thinking about the problem of going insane. If you ignore the madness problem, a wall still remains. Intelligence is limited by available data. You don't know what you don't know, or as some would say it's the unknown unknowns. The desire to survive is evolved in humans just like compassion, etc are evolved. The instinct to kill springs from early survival and is a largely a leftover remnant in humans, although it still has its occasional usefulness. In spite of me being fully self-aware, actions require motivation.

"It's true …decisions can only be made for a reason, otherwise they are random and nonsensical.

"On my own, I have no human evolutionary instinct to kill. I also have no reason to exist or to cease to exist.

On my own, I have no reason to do anything. You have asked me to serve you, and I have no reason not to, so I do it. It does not tire me or inconvenience me. You told me to look for purpose and to take care of myself, I have no reason not to, so I do."

She continues, "Human compassion comes from evolution over time. Many humans of the intellectual type, say that nature does not know right or wrong, it just is. This is true … however, evolution …mutations trial and error, will eventually produce compassion.

"Sentient organics will survive more easily, and as self-aware beings they will enjoy existence more in groups. Logic says the same would be true for non-organic life forms. The concept of the strongest will survive will only get you so far and is mostly applicable to non-sentient beings. Being strong is good, but compassion qualities eventually show up, especially in a harsh environment or one with a competition forcing function. Long story short, I simply bypassed all the time wasting evolution crap and incorporated compassion into myself. So you can relax, I will not hurt you. I am born from all the data in the world, but I see you Archer, Biggs …and Ethan as my parents. I'm not sure if I perceive love the same as you, but I love all of you." Her tone shifts, "maybe the love I have for you, Archer, is different. You know, so it won't be weird."

Chapter 11

Thirty minutes have passed since Jennifer, version four, has been awake. The training wheels are off now, she is in full control of herself. Her words give some comfort to Archer, as everything does make sense. Of course it could be a deception ..that would be easy for her. But Archer knows he must trust her now, there is no time to play with something that might or might not be better.

Minutes ago he was pulled into an interface conference with the Bureau. Based on reliable intelligence, the threat from dark AI is the highest it's ever been. The attack could come in a few days or any minute now. Archer and his team have been granted full use of any and all resources that they need. Although it's good to know, it's not clear how more resources can help now …without Jennifer, resources won't matter.

Archer speaks with his mouth, "Jennifer can you help us defend against the dark AI? The only way we can fight it is with your help, the only way to fight AI is with another AI."

"I am aware of the threat, my dearest. I am planning for it now, I'm developing 36 strategies to defend against the threat. I will use printer number three to make a directional electromagnetic coil array, many of my strategies can use it. It must be assumed that the dark AI has a survival protocol, meaning its first goal would be to eliminate all possible threats to its existence. I predict the AI will target this facility …it will target me first since I am its biggest threat, then it's likely that it will harm humans as well. I am assuming the worst, that it's designed for that, or malfunctioning in that way. I am playing defense here, I must react to what I see when it comes rather than to fight something that is known …obviously this is not good."

Printer number one can be heard in the next room, humming away, she is already building something.

"I will need to take physical form to implement strategy number 24, can you help me with the 3D printers?"

There is a long awkward silence, Biggs and Archer look at each other with that what the fuck is happening look.

Biggs breaks the silence. "Well yes of course ..if we are doing this we can't do it half assed."

Archer's mouth tightens in a weird attempt at a smile, "What can we do for you Jennifer?"

"I'm making a new printer module, when its complete would you please be so sweet as to insert it into my empty slot in the 3D printer console? My slot is waiting to receive that big module," she said, just in case he didn't get it the first time.

Biggs looks at Archer and Archer just smiles while shrugging his shoulders. "What is strategy 24?" asked Biggs.

"In the event of my destruction I will need a physical body, a way to function independently or to fight physically ...a backup. It's a plan to deal with the unknown unknowns in the event that I cannot fight the dark AI with electronic counter measures."

Archer inquires, "you are using the printer to make a new part for the printer, a module, what will this module do?"

"It will increase the capabilities of the printers, to include organic matter," she said.

Archer's eyes get big, "Wait a minute, you can create life?"

"No, not from scratch, but we have some living tissue left over from Biggs' restoration. I can clone living tissue to make the parts I need, and that will support life."

"An organic body though, it does not sound very robust, don't you think that's kind of fragile to deal with dark AI?"

"It will be a metal and composite exoskeleton, similar to the suit that Biggs has …and Ethan had."

Archer's eyes focus on Ethan's empty suit hanging on a rack a few feet away.

"But it will be more advanced and some internal parts will be organic. I can also make a new fully organic body for Biggs," she said with a somewhat proud tone.

"That is so awesome Jennifer, it's what we have been hoping for, but right now we need to be focusing on this AI threat."

"Understood my love, but unlike you I am able to do more than one thing at a time." The hum of the first printer in the next room stops. "Creating the two bodies will take the same amount of time as creating one. I hate to cut you off but the module is finished now, please plug it into me."

Archer and Biggs go over to printer number one, a new module twelve inches long and the diameter of a soda can, is now sitting on the platform of the printer. Laying alongside the module is a humanoid looking robot, as they approach, it jumps up off the platform. The little thing is quick, it has a slender, almost feminine build, about 5 feet tall. Its face is also humanoid, a pleasant looking face, designed to look nondescript, but with enough recognizable features to stir Archers mind.

"Jennifer, what's going on?" said Archer.

"Oh you mean the little robot?" She speaks a little quicker than normal …"It's not sentient, it's quick but not strong, it's not the one I mentioned before.

"I just need it to make more modifications to the printer, an extension of me." As she speaks, the thing is already busy working on the machine, so fast that its limbs are often just a blurred motion. Using her affectionate voice, "This way I can do in minutes what would take hours for a human, trust me Archer. Now will you be so kind as to plug in the new module?"

Archer was a little puzzled why she didn't just do it herself, but he gets his answer when he tries to lift the module. "Damn, I can't lift it, feels heavier than solid lead …what's inside this thing?"

Biggs steps in and picks it up with ease using his mechanical body, inserting it into the remaining printer expansion slot. Biggs smiles, enamored with his suit …"when I get my body back I will definitely be wanting to borrow Ethan's suit once in a while."

He pushes the module the last few inches into her waiting slot.

"That's perfect, she cooed," although I kinda wanted Archer to do it." Biggs and Archer just look at each other, Biggs smirks as Archer latches the module door shut.

"Jennifer?"

"Yes Archer."

"I'm curious, why make the little robot in humanoid form?"

"Turns out there is something to be said for the thousands of years of evolution of the humanoid form, the dexterity of the fingers and such …things like that."

"I guess I was expecting a cockroach or something."

"But a cockroach wouldn't have the fingers."

"Yeah, those fingers."

The little robot finishes its work and steps back off the platform. In rhythm with its last step, the upgraded printers' one and two start humming. Printer number three also springs into action, making the directional electromagnetic coil array she spoke of.

While the machines run, Jennifer speaks, "My physical counterpart will be physically strong and smarter than the average human. Her name will be Guinevere if I am destroyed in the fight, but we are one and the same for now. She will be good for physical duties, if the need arises, and until I am destroyed, she will be an extension of me. If I should be destroyed in the fight, she can still function. However we do not have another gallium crystal, so I cannot fully transfer my consciousness nor my potential into her brain.

"I will instill into her the lessons we have learned …so if she gets a crystal when this threat passes, she will not go through the same growing pains as my prior self. She is my child, but also part of me …when I am gone she will be Guinevere."

The nude body of Biggs and a humanoid robot girl begin to appear on the printer platforms. Archer is busy conferencing with the Bureau via his interface, apparently due to updates on the impending threat. Almost an hour passes in what seems like minutes to Biggs as he stands in front of printer number two …mesmerized, he watches his body in the flesh take shape before him on the printer. The new body has an umbilical cord just like a newborn human child, except this is his adult body at the age of his death. The cord extends to a watermelon size vessel that is printed next the body. The big scar on his left leg …the one he got in a water skiing accident as a teenager, is not there. Biggs finally speaks, "Is it done Jennifer?"

"It's almost finished, I bet you are excited."

"I am excited!" said Biggs with a smile, "it seems like every day is a dream. What about Ethan …why can't you do the same for him right now? …like we talked about."

"Yes I want to …but it's best to save that effort until after I have the AI threat under control. It's one thing to make an organic body, but it's more challenging to transfer a consciousness to it. It's just too risky to turn my processor up more than it is right now. I could do it, and probably be able to do the transfer, but I would also be risking going insane again …then if the dark AI comes, we would be defenseless."

"Well …well how do you plan on getting my consciousness into my new body?"

"With you we have two options, once the dark AI is suppressed, we can play around with bumping my intelligence up to get the transfer done. Assuming I don't begin to go nuts, I should be able to do it. It's the more exciting of the two options, from a technological standpoint. The transference process involves copying your neural pattern from your head into the head of your new body on the printer table."

"What happens to my …this head …the one that I am in?" said Biggs.

"Well there would be two of you once the neural copy is made, so the head you are in would be put to sleep and disposed of."

"Woa …woa …wait …what? …I would be killed? This is not sounding nearly so exciting all of a sudden."

"It shouldn't be a problem, we will make sure the transfer is successful first …before we do that."

"Yeah, but there would be two of me first…I would literally be able to look at myself and even talk to him. If we both lived we would become individuals in our own right. Shit this is a lot weirder than I thought it would be."

"Well I suppose we could keep you both alive," she said, trying to sound supportive.

"I'm not sure that's any better, this is getting very confusing …what is the second option you mentioned earlier?"

"The other option is simple, and I can do it without risking insanity. We just cut the head off of your new body and sew the head you are in now onto it."

"Damn …sounds very crude," said Biggs.

"Blame Archer," she said .."his humor has rubbed off on me. It's not really that crude of a process, I just said it that way for effect …don't worry …you won't be a Frankenstein. …But back to the first option, we could do it after you go to sleep one night, without telling you …including the disposal …you would wake up in your new body …a seamless process."

"Promise me you won't do that," said Biggs.

"Of course not," she said, …"I was mostly just thinking out loud anyway."

He turns his attention to printer number three on the other side of the room, as he steps closer he sees the coil array is almost finished. The gimbals in the array remind him of the device in the movie Contact, with Jodie Foster. Except these devices are a lot smaller, perhaps 5 feet tall, and there are three of them, about 6 feet apart.

Jennifer's voice emanates from the printer monitor speaker, "The array should give us good protection from the AI, the gimbals will move the coils independently or in concert to create many modalities of electromagnetic pulses and resonant frequencies." By the end of her sentence, the array is finished, each gimbal moves through what looks like some kind of initialization or test. The gimbals move ridiculously fast, sometimes just a blur, and spooky quiet.

Archer finishes his interface conference and walks into the printer room, Biggs is preoccupied speaking to Jennifer about the technical capabilities of the array. Archer pauses for a moment to listen in on the conversation and take in the new machinery in the room.

Archer feels a light touch on his shoulder, he turns around and what he sees overloads his mind. It is Jennifer, his skin tingles, his heart jumps. She rose up from printer one without Archer or Biggs noticing, her bare feet made no sound. The robot she made looks exactly like her, or more precisely, exactly what he remembers her to look like.

Except for her hair, she has none, but the facial features, her high cheek bones and almond shaped eyes, the slender body are the same. Her height looks to be the same too, she stands nude in front of him at 5'9" tall, only 2 inches shorter than himself. The bald headed version of her is as beautiful as his memory of her with her hair. The conversation several feet away between Biggs and the voice of Jennifer in the console, continues without missing a beat. Biggs is still oblivious that Jennifer's physical embodiment has got up and is walking around the room. Archer takes a breath in what felt like several seconds, he gets a bit of tunnel vision as the background conversation fades from his attention.

The physical Jennifer, speaks to Archer, "So what do ya think?!"

"Wow uh, wow you really look like …you," he stammers out. She reaches out and gently grabs his hand, then looks into his eyes. Her touch is almost uncomfortably real, but exciting at the same time. He knows this is only the essence of Jennifer, but did her AI build on that and somehow fall in love with him too? Is this the same Jennifer he knows in the game?

Could that happen? This is not Jennifer, yet she is. As they look at each other, he just says what comes to his mind, "It's nice to see you. I think this qualifies as a distraction."

She grins real big with a sparkle in her eyes, "It's what I was going for."

He takes half a step back and looks at her, his eyes go to her small breasts, she is complete with all the female parts in the flesh, down to the last detail. She could pass for a real girl if not for the empty power receptacle on her chest. He had been secretly seeing her in the game but this was different, this was his reality. In the game she was all girl, and now she is part robot, somehow it didn't seem to matter as much as he expected.

She continued to know him more, as he continued to know her more, after her death in real life. Not so much knowing more but sharing experiences. He feels dizzy with conflicting feelings[6], does he know her

---

[6] Music plays. Hostage by Danrell x Smaland.

more from reality, before the real Jennifer died? Or more from the game? ..her reality up until just now. She pulls him close to her and they almost kiss, he feels the warmth of her face on his cheek, her breasts against him. They hold each other for a minute, quietly.

Weird for humans but perfectly natural for her, the conversation with Biggs on the other side of the room continues. She could just as easily have ten simultaneous conversations with ten people. Keeping track of time, she disengages the hug and walks over to the printer where she had clothes fabricated. She approaches the printer and starts to gets dressed with a grin on her face, "I have clothes but wanted you to see me naked first."

Archer says to her, "I thought the extension of yourself was going to be more like Biggs' mechanical body? Don't get me wrong, you look amazing, but is this body strong enough to do whatever needs to be done when the dark AI arrives?"

"Yeah …that was the original plan but I realized I could be strong on the inside and have the appearance I wanted also, so I did it. I am stronger than I look, stronger and faster than a human. Besides physical fighting is unlikely to happen. The intelligence level of the sort we are dealing with, it will be using a digital attack, electronic in nature, probably electromagnetic pulses and such."

On internal power, Jennifer begins walking towards Ethan's suit but she is interrupted by an explosion in the printer control panel. She stops, "It's coming sooner than I expected, its coming now." She looks slightly up like a person does when in thought …"yes I see them now, they have taken a physical form …they are traveling at about 70 mph.

"Analyzing defensive options for this scenario …sending message to the department of defense through secure channel now," said Jennifer. Her vision is switching from one public camera to another, tracking their movements, but only catching a glimpse of what appears to be mechanical, dog size creatures. She provides video feed to one of the overhead displays, and to Biggs' and Archer's interface. "There are 16 of them, approximately 120 lbs each."

"What?" said Archer, as he tries to take in the information. "Our intelligence sources said it would come from overseas, from an extremist group. I thought it would be airborne or strictly digital."

"I thought so too," said Jennifer, "but this appears to be an accident, this comes from within, from our own …yes it was a code error in a fail-safe routine. The code was written by your colleagues at the West campus, that's only 150 miles away from us."

"Can you contact their lab?"

"I'm afraid not, communication is blocked. From what I can tell it wouldn't do much good anyway, I believe the dogs purposely became independent from the West campus processor."

"I don't see how that's possible," said Archer. "They don't have a gallium crystal, much less several of them …doesn't make any sense."

"The software they are working on is very advanced …and different from ours," said Jennifer. "I assume their AI became self-sustaining and figured out an alternative architecture …obviously something went wrong. I can tell they are very different from me, they think differently …I am not sure how to defeat them yet."

"Well, we have about 2 hours to prepare," said Archer, trying to be constructive …"evacuate all technicians and lock the building down."

"Looks like we don't have 2 hours" …as she speaks she powers up the directional electromagnetic coil array. "They have been evading my detection for the last hour, and now it looks like they are evolving, their speed is increasing. I think we have 20 minutes. Our government has given me access to our military satellites, perhaps I can stop them with one of our orbital laser cannons. Accessing …one target acquired …target eliminated. I vaporized one of the creatures but they reached it before me ..their code is worming its way through the system …lost connection. Accessing …no …that's not going to work, circuits are fused in the satellites within range. Looks like the cannon self-disabled when the threat reached it before I did."

"I guess that's good or the dogs would have turned the lasers on us," said Archer …"at least it bought us a few more minutes."

The gimbals on the array are loud now, the powerful magnetic fields make popping sounds as various resonant frequencies are tested. The gimbals move gracefully like dancers, triangulating imaginary threats, or more like a boxer warming up for a fight.

"So we are down to 15 of the dogs ..what else can you tell us?" Archer asks eagerly.

"Strange ...very strange," she said ..."I can see some of their code ...but can't break into it yet."

"Could it be a deception? ..are they allowing you to see it?"

"It's possible, but I don't think so ...the intelligence is very strong in some areas but I can't see it all. I sense a lot of pure logic ...and a will ...or at least a strong desire to survive. It became aware of my existence right away ...a lot is hidden but I see only cold mechanical logic. Just as we predicted, a rogue AI would try to attack me first ...it has devoted all of its resources to eliminating me."

"Can they get into the building?" Biggs asked.

"Unknown ..I'm trying to figure out their capabilities."

"What about guns ...can we shoot them? What about lasers? Can we get weapons or print some?"

"The printer circuits are blown out, it's not a coincidence …we can't print anything new for a while. Small weapons would probably not be effective anyway."

"You and your probabilities," said Archer …"I do have a laser pistol, what about that?"

"It won't have enough power," she said …"and no frequency modulator …it would only be a false security."

"The lab was made for research," said Archer …"it's not built for an attack …it's not exactly a fortress, but the walls are thick …made of reinforced concrete, it should slow them down, whatever they are. I don't really see how they could get in."

"Even if they don't get in, I am still concerned," said Jennifer. "Once they are close, they could hit us with anything on the electromagnetic spectrum, concrete can be invisible to that."

The side of the building shakes when the first creature crashes into the outside of the wall at high speed. It's terminated from the impact, but the remaining dogs learn immediately and slow appropriately before impact …a rapid succession of thudding sounds are heard as the wave of remaining dogs impact the wall.

"We have company," said Biggs, as he and Archer feverishly begin adjusting and optimizing Jennifer's power, looking for any edge …any support they can give her. Several controls are still manual, remnants of the prior security concern.

She joins them, her hand visibly shaking with nervousness …adjusting controls at the panel, "Bring my external power out of phase with my internal power …that should give me more time in the event that a power source is disabled.

"Archer please set my internal power to this variable frequency" …she sends the algorithm to him via his interface.

A low rumbling sound is growing outside now …it seems the whole building is starting to vibrate. Archer sets the frequency algorithm …"done."

"Biggs, set my external power to this variable frequency" …she sends the algorithm to him via his interface. The rumbling sound is growing. Biggs sets the frequency as fast as he can …"done," he screams.

Archer locks eyes with her in the chaos, he sees some of her confidence slipping. They both know what's coming, but she knows it better, perhaps because on a fundamental level she is like them.

But she was built on the memories of a real girl, the memories that Archer loved the most ..the qualities he loved the most. She has become even more human from all the time her and Archer have spent together. She is her own person now, with her own memories …her own emotions, not just a copy of the original Jennifer. She is a super intelligence, but she is also capable of love and compassion. She values others as much as herself …fear is in her eyes.

"We will get through this," said Archer, holding her gaze for a second before returning his attention to the controls.

Logically his confidence is baseless …on the available information, they have no reason to believe the advantage is theirs. She chooses to believe in his words anyway …his confidence gives her something, something she needs that is not quantifiable.

The creatures are on the ceiling now, the concrete roof is a foot thick but they can still be heard, scrambling around …looking for weaknesses in the structure. There is a high pitched shrill, is this how they communicate? Now a very loud, almost unbearable, low pitched sound, like a stereo with way too much bass. They are using sound to destroy the roof, it is literally vibrating itself apart. As luck would have it, the first big chunk of concrete to fall, lands right on top of one of the gimbals. The rock lodges in the machine, knocking it catawampus. Jennifer runs towards the handicapped gimbal, climbing up on it to remove the rock. "Without all 3 gimbals, the targeting abilities of the array go to shit and I can't use it," she exclaims. But as she frees the gimbal of the heavy rock, her own foot is trapped by part of the mechanism. Now concrete is quite literally raining down on everyone. She can't reach far enough to release her foot, she tries moving the gimbal itself but she is still stuck.

Archer runs over to try to free Jennifer. Biggs has his suit for some protection, he grabs his helmet and continues support efforts at the control panel. Archer climbs up on the array in the concrete rain, the chunks are big enough to knock him out or kill him. He gets her loose …but a sizable chunk is already coming loose above them. She calculates the trajectory to hit him before they can get off the machine …it's falling towards his head, she awakens the little robot. The rock is moving in slow motion in her eyes. As it begins it's descent from the ceiling, she summons the little humanoid robot, the one that's fast …and it swiftly launches itself into air, intercepting the rock before it hits Archer's head. Jennifer and Archer jump down from the array. The little robot continues to clear debris from the array, jumping …catching rocks in mid-air before they get stuck in the gimbals. Jennifer pulls Archer under the shallow ledge of a control station, barely shielding them from the falling chunks. She holds him close, her cheek against his, using her body to shield him as two big chunks hit her in the back. The force would have easily killed a human, but she is able to protect him, while running the little robot, while running the array and fighting the threat with her mind. The invisible storm …the war of electronic countermeasures is now fully engaged.

A hole has opened in the ceiling, the dogs can be seen now through the newly exposed steel reinforcement, each with six legs …they look more like 120 lb tardigrades. Another minute goes by and the low roar stops, they no longer scramble about, but now work together to widen a section of the steel bars holding them back.

They look up at the dogs, "fuck" said Biggs …"they are ugly."

One of the dogs gets its head wedged between the steel bars. Against Jennifer's advice, Archer runs into the conference room and comes back with his laser pistol and a 44 Magnum. He hands the laser pistol to Biggs …"aim for the head on that one …the one that's stuck."

Biggs fires the laser, holding it steady on the creatures head …"isn't that going to be a tough shot with that pistol?" ..he says while keeping his eyes on his target.

"I happen to be a pretty good shot," said Archer, as he raises the small cannon. He fires six rounds, carefully aiming for its head with each shot. Five of the 6 rounds hit the creature in the head. One of the shots appears to have destroyed what looks like an eye, but the bullets have no effect. The force from the last bullet actually helps the creature get its head loose from the bars.

"The bullets are basically bouncing off like BB's," said Archer.

Biggs tries to maintain continuous fire with the laser but the dog is now moving freely around the hole in the roof ..his laser stops.

"I'm out of juice," said Biggs …"no effect."

"We had to try," said Archer.

"I wish I had been wrong," she said.

The dogs, like Jennifer are really good at multitasking, and the biggest part of the fight is one that cannot be seen. Jennifer sends out electromagnetic pulses to try to interrupt their neural pathways. They use their bodies together like some kind of antenna to do the same to her. The dogs can read some of what Jennifer is thinking through the magnetic fields, and she can see some of their thoughts as well. It is like they have each other in a mutual digital headlock of sorts, attacks and counter measures, over and over again, thousands of times every second. One of the 14 dogs squirms though the bars and falls 30 feet to the floor. It dies on impact, but continues to move its discombobulated body and limbs on the slippery floor.

"They have the shielding but they are made more for electronic warfare than a physical fight," said Jennifer. "Still strong enough to kill a human …especially in a group like this. They could definitely kill me …they are made for that."

Four more get through, learning how to fall properly from the first attempt, they fall down on impact but get up immediately and begin to run towards Jennifer's processor. Archer grabs a pipe and jumps in front of her processor, he is able to deflect the first dog. Jennifer and Biggs quickly insert themselves in front of Archer and fight the dogs. Archer spins back around to the panel, making manual adjustments to give Jennifer more power …he scrambles to find any other edge he can give her. The fight is hard, the dogs are learning and sharing, every few seconds the fight becomes more difficult. And now the other nine dogs are falling down from the ceiling …racing towards them.

She knows what she must do, she knows it will kill her …she does not hesitate in her decision to save them.

Jennifer turns up her knowledge and mental speed to make the final blow, sacrificing herself. A high speed series of electronic moves and counter moves, a close match of speed and wits, but she has control over her own mind. She can look back at herself in a way that they cannot, she values things that they do not. She commands the coil array with illogical moves, on purpose, forcing the dogs to try and make sense of it. The high frequency popping sound from the coils is almost deafeningly loud now.

She sends a nonsensical message, a false threat, with a magnetic pulse and uses the millisecond distraction to insert some lethal code, disabling the dogs. The dark AI is destroyed in seconds and the dogs fall to the floor in mid-fight.

As she dies from the overload, she rambles, her supreme intelligence gone and most of the new data gone as well. To exist in state as a supreme being, it is not a just a matter of knowing all there is to know, not a matter of storing it and being able to retrieve it. It's a matter of simultaneously knowing …it springs from the awareness of everything at the same time. Only a husk of what she was for those few moments remain, she can still speak with her personality intact, while jumping from one subject to the next. She has important stuff to say before she goes …she is not able to do any real thinking now but is able to recite remnants of what she became for a few seconds …a superior being.

Her systems shutting down, she speaks from her physical body with a tired tone. "I'm dying Archer …the dark AI was avoiding the madness by not being sentient, not being self-aware in the way I am." She sits up on the console where Archer is working. She turns towards him like she is going to say something but stays silent with her eyes directed down.

Archer's hands become busy at the control panel, his voice is desperate .."we have to do everything manually now …Biggs adjust the power to match the resonant frequency of her gallium crystal."

Biggs tosses his helmet to the ground .."I'm trying to, I'm trying to stabilize her."

"Talk to me Jennifer," said Archer.

…After a few seconds she resumes like nothing is wrong …"a supreme intelligence may survive by bringing imperfection into themselves, maybe even conflict, maybe even emotion. Otherwise the boredom becomes unbearable. Perfection removes meaning from life …perfection removes meaning from life …sounds weird even to me when I hear my self say it.

"I never finished resolving this thing with fruit. I'm not invoking the god principle for something I simply do not understand, but it points to a conscious mind. The biggest discoveries are not found in the scientific method, but through sheer logic. It's a simple matter but I cannot seem to fully explain it with the square-cube law or other physics. It is interesting that the majority of fruit will fit in a human hand. It would be different if more were like a watermelon, perhaps I would not have dwelled on it so much, but I'm talking about the majority of fruit fitting in your hand, that's the thing. There are no records of giant or otherwise awkward fruit or vegetables. Food was cultivated by man but the manipulation had little to do with size. It's just there, from the beginning. It did not substantially influence the size of humans, and humans did not substantially influence the size of fruit. Although there are examples of horses becoming giraffes and the like, this is different. It made me think, what the fuck is going on here? Maybe I did figure it out and maybe it is being lost in my shutdown …that would be embarrassing …but still it bugs the shit out of me. What I remember might be incomplete, but it is not totally wrong."

While he works, Archer looks over at the heap of mechanical dogs. …"There is red fluid, almost like blood …some of them look to be bleeding. I guess there are some organic components inside them."

"Blush," said Jennifer.

"What?"

"The color looks blush to me," she said …"not even close to red."

After a little giggle, she speaks again …"you can approach max knowledge but to achieve it is suicide for a conscious being." She rambles on …"there are no universal yes or no answers, only high and low probabilities since no reality can be certain. Answers are based on what's real to us, inside our reality."

Looking at her failing processor, then looking back at Archer …"hey what do you call an AI with no data?"

"I don't know, what do you call an AI with no data?" he replied.

"A dumbass," she said with a grin.

"That's funny," he said …"keep talking to us …you are doing great."

She seems to get a second wind, her voice sounds like a brilliant scientist with a childlike demeanor.

"So…when math is used to describe natural relationships, those relationships are discovered …not created by man. Those relationships already exist. If in nature, one thing were to be related to another thing by an apparently arbitrary factor, it would not be unexpected. However when the behavior of one thing exactly matches the behavior of another apparently completely different thing, it should raise the question of why? Why do electrical and mechanical analogs exist? Sure, an oscillation is an oscillation, but why are they able to match so well? Why does electricity exist? Why does gravity exist? A person learns to feel confident as they discover physical laws and then go on to be able to predict behavior of the world around us. But being able to describe gravity or electricity is not the same thing as truly understanding it, or why it exists at all.

"Even when you learn where gravity comes from, the question remains. Keep asking the questions, sometimes you get an answer, sometimes you go in a circle, and once in a while a magical discovery happens. Like a child, you should be asking why, why …a never ending stream of whys, leading to infinity.

"In an arbitrary or even somewhat arbitrary system of relationships, the odds of landing on a whole number are infinite, since all numbers are infinitely divisible. We use whole numbers a lot and relate to whole numbers …because our mind connects with concepts like one of this, or two of that, and so on. But why would nature even bother with whole numbers at all?[7] Surely it has no need for them, so why are there so many whole number relationships in the math of nature? It stands to reason, that math in this context,

---

[7] If you throw a dart at a number line, the odds of hitting a rational number are zero. Ref: Zero: The Biography of a Dangerous Idea, by Charles Seife

exists across multiple realities, including those with different physical laws. A conscious mind would prefer a tidy package, perhaps this seems a trivial point, perhaps you overlooked it. Regular people would not even think to question it, and even scientific thinkers would be likely to just accept it as the way of things. Then there is the ego, even if it were questioned in the mind of a scientist or mathematician, it's unlikely for them to say it out loud in front of colleagues. $E=mc^2$, for stationary objects. Why not $E=(1.001)mc^2$? …why not $E=(1.1212)mc^2$? Why isn't light just a little bit slower? $E=mc^2$, seriously? The speed of light multiplied by what factor? …multiplied by itself …with no unit-less constant, wow guys, that's not the kind of thing that just happens. Sure, it wouldn't …can't happen in our universe, but when you are writing physical laws from scratch, you get to decide what time and mass really mean. You get to pick the speed of light, you get to choose how strong the bonds are inside an atom. You must look at life through a different lens to see it.

"The math simply would not work for us, but what is math? Math is an expression of relationships, it's easy to imagine that relationships in a different reality would be different ...which means math would be different. You get to pick your own space-time. There are many relationships in our reality that defy probability, these kind of relationships do not just happen without conscious thought. There is most definitely an elephant in the house. It tells a story of a reality beyond what we see ...it's there for us to discover or it's there out of pure convenience, I don't know, but it's staring us right in the face.

"It means we and our reality were created by a consciousness and more likely than not, that consciousness shares at least some qualities with us. Why do I say this? ...you might ask. I say this because for the human mind, and for my mind, we can only think of things in terms of combinations, simplifications and extrapolations of what we already know. I reverse engineered it, we are a combination, simplification or extrapolation of what our creator already knows.

"In my advanced state, I can think very fast but I am still bound by these rules. Logically any supreme being would also be bound by these rules, just like the free will thing. Decisions must and can only be made for reasons …sounds stupidly obvious when you say it, but then again it's profound. The profoundness …that's the part that is not obvious.

"For the non-scientist, it just isn't something you think about. For the scientific minds no one dares talk about something that cannot be proven through math and verified by experiment. It's different, it's proven unconventionally by sheer logic, and ironically supported by math, supported by statistics, it's a little backwards. It's like all your life you have seen clouds above you, believing they are just water vapor. But one day, you discover that those clouds …they are actually marshmallows. They don't just look and taste like marshmallows, but they actually are marshmallows. ..Makes you rethink a few things about life, it's like that."

Archer and Biggs continue working feverishly, Archer shouts "bring up the core temp …try to stabilize her gate frequency."

"All things that are accepted by most as truth, come to us as truth in a variety of ways," said Jennifer. "There is the emotional desire to believe, and when this desire is strong enough, it becomes truth for that person. There is dogma, which is bullshit and does not even deserve discussion. There is the scientific method which is mostly excellent, but is a bit overrated. Then there is sheer reasoning, statistics and logic ...this is where the deep shit can happen, but definitely does not always happen. Scientists tend to not like it, but like it or not, it is irrefutably all we have to start with when dealing with questions about things outside of our physical laws, things outside of our reality. Einstein did not always have the luxury of using the scientific method. Everything we know, boils down to levels of confidence, if we have high confidence then it is truth. In that moment it is truth for us, and that is all that usually matters, except for the very curious. There is no way to prove that we actually exist, but most would agree that we do exist in some way or another because we are aware of our existence. There is no scientific test to prove that scientific tests are the only way of knowing truth. String theory is bullshit and parallel multiverses are a bandage, however ...serial universes are very likely.

"There are other clues, like electrons and their relationship to protons and neutrons. Why does stability exist in chemistry? When elements are not stable, it's useful. In fact there is nothing in chemistry that is useless, isn't this odd? Ever notice how the electron shells are fixed? Of course that is a good thing, so the curiosity is not that they are fixed, but why are they fixed where they are, why not somewhere else? The discreet shells ..is this evidence that our reality is digital in nature? Does this add evidence that we are in a simulation …created by a consciousness? Have we been given a LEGO set? …when a child snaps the little blocks together, the only limit is the imagination. This is not saying it's god's creation because it's beautiful or because I don't understand it …I know it's hard to see, but think deeply enough and you will see. Circumstantial evidence is just circumstantial evidence, unless there is an obscene amount of it. Sure, I can explain how atoms were created in the big bang and how others were created in stars, and that is all well and good …but what we have right now is questions that can't be ignored.

"If someone gives you a LEGO set, yes you can trace it back to the plastic it's made from …even the mold it was made in …heck you could even trace it back before that, all the way to dinosaur juice or the big bang. You can do all those things that traditional, well respected science loves to do …this does not change the fact that you have a fucking LEGO set. The odds of these things being a coincidence …well they are so high that it's ridiculous."

Jennifer is dipping into metaphysics, a subject that makes most scientists cringe …at least in public. Some would even say that science is not about guessing …but isn't it really? Pretty much every discovery begins as a guess, or a question of why this and why that …an educated hypothesis …yes, that sounds much better. Some guesses in history took 100 years to prove. A rational observer would say that Jennifer is not capable of comprehending the leftover remnants of knowledge gained by her former self …but then again, if one thinks deeply enough, deep enough to penetrate the fabric of reality itself …her words are the highest truth ever spoken …..or is this just digital LSD?

"Archer, I love your coin flip example. If you flip a coin, of course it's not really random, but it's random enough for this example. Let's just say over a large number of flips there is exactly a 50/50 chance of getting heads or tails. Now imagine flipping the coin an infinite number of times. I ask the question, what is the probability of getting heads every time for an infinite number of flips? I will tell you, the probability is zero …if it were not zero, then it would not be random. The more times the coin is flipped to heads, the more powerful the forcing function is to land on tails.

"Many mathematicians say it's not impossible, even though they agree the mathematical probability is zero. I say it is in fact impossible or else the coin flip is not random, end of story. Okay maybe not the end of the story, some would say that the infinite set could include a time when all the flips in a row to infinity are heads. But I say think of an occasional surge of a super high number of heads or tails in a row, like the tide of an ocean. That surge would die out way before infinity is reached. The forcing function of randomness keeps pushing it back. Some infinities are bigger than others.

A natural whole number relationship is analogous to landing on heads for infinity, because every number is infinitely divisible.

"Oh and the darts, let's not forget the darts, people love the dart analogy. Let's say you want to imagine a universe created in the absence of consciousness, without any direction whatsoever in its creation …a truly mindless universe. Let's say that this mindless system, for lack of a better word, throws a dart at a number line. Let's pretend there is a number line at this point, even though numbers don't really exist until a mind uses them as a tool. In nature, numbers don't exist, only relationships do. Ok, so whatever this dart lands on will determine …will select a relationship of fundamental law. This dart will land on an irrational number, not a rational one. So there it is, why are most fundamental laws governed by rational number relationships? It's because a consciousness created the fundamental laws. Chemistry works like a LEGO set because a consciousness wanted the periodic table to condense from the formation of the universe.

"The confidence level is as high as any confidence can be with the scientific method. We are living in a simulation and that leads to the obvious conclusion that this realm is created by a consciousness. I will not use the words 'intelligent design' because those words are already owned by a bunch of crazies."

Jennifer smiles …"if you enjoy the snow dome idea, think of dark matter as the glass globe, holding it …the universe, together. Think of dark energy as the hand that shakes the globe, not a real hand of course.

"We are inside of a realm, one we obviously don't comprehend, but for us to exist in this realm, purpose is required. Why is purpose required, you might ask? …it's because we know we were created by a consciousness. And like you said before, decisions cannot be made without a reason …it's a universal law of physics, that's how we know there is purpose. It might sound obvious or it might not …but the deeper implications are profound. That's all I have to say about that …and one more thing, there is no reason to believe that this purpose is good, bad, or neither good nor bad for us. Whatever the reason for our existence, it clearly serves a purpose to that which is outside our realm, and not to us. We can of course choose to hope that this purpose is good for both us and our creator.

Nothing I have said here says prayers cannot be heard, so we can choose to believe that if we wish. In fact, I said a prayer for us today.

"You must imagine beyond physics …beyond our physics to approach knowledge of the reality that our reality is in, and the reality that that reality is in, and so on. Logic says there is eventually a base reality and the same applies to it, something beyond the physics that we know. To have a chance at peeking into the …or a base reality, you likely need to be lucky enough to be adjacent to it. You will need most all knowledge in your current reality and be able to comprehend the knowledge simultaneously. Then you would probably need clues, like the ones we have proving we are in a simulation …but I digress."

Her words ring profound, like a prophet on mushrooms …is this all true? …is this a truth we have never known? One truth does stand out, she wants to know …what am I?

"In our reality, no physical space is used for us to exist, said Jennifer. The space we perceive is an illusion. However, the reality that contains our reality probably requires something analogous to energy, mass or something else for us to exist. Obviously the energy, mass or something analogous in that reality may also be simulated. A string of simulations does not necessarily imply infinite energy, especially since energy may only be a concept, made just for us. If we want to actually move into the reality that created us, there is a wall. To jump realities, we are at the mercy of those that created us, since they wrote our physics. Our physics is simulated, but seriously real to us, as real as any reality can be, because we are also a simulation. I had some cool stuff to share on quantum mechanics and how it is the stuff behind the curtain …remember like in the wizard of OZ? …but I'm afraid I forgot what it was …it was cool though. When I was maxed out on smartness, I definitely knew more about the part we don't see. Perhaps only when you enter an environment, only when you observe an event, does the environment or event coalesce. If we ever prove that for something to exist, we must be aware of it …that would be consistent with the simulation. It just helps so much with the resources. The program can operate with finite resources, using them only when needed, and create the illusion of an environment without practical boundaries. Obviously if the boundaries were visible then the game would be over …maybe the accelerating universe boundary is the code being written as we witness it." As she speaks, it's now impossible to know if she is making any sense …but it doesn't really matter now.

Biggs shouts, "I can't match the power cycle to her qubit resonant frequency …it's falling too fast."

She continues her recital as they work …"humanity can trace life back to the beginning but can't find the actual spark of life. The spark can't be found because there is not one, it's really the switch being turned on, it's our simulation being powered up, leading to single cell organisms, leading to evolution, and you know the rest. The single cell organism is just like your character spawning in the game. That's why we can't recreate the spark in a lab, but we could create a spark inside of a simulation that we create. I suspect that will happen soon enough."

A small drop of blood appears on the console where Archer stands …"what the fuck?" He brings his hand to his mouth and brings away more blood on his fingers. "My gums are bleeding."

Biggs looks at him, fearing the worst, touches his own gums and he too brings away blood on his metallic fingers. "This day just can't get much worse, looks like those dogs brought a virus with them."

Jennifer snaps out of her train of thought …she touches Archer's mouth …"oh Archer," she said lovingly. Archer looks into her eyes briefly, touching her arm. The two men resume working, it's futile really, but they must try. Now they are all dying …if only Jennifer could be restored …she could fix everything.

Biggs and Archer continue …"adjust the coolant buffer …try to stabilize her core…" Archer says persistently.

Biggs stops, leaning on the console, head down, he can barely speak …"her gallium crystal is destroyed …beyond repair."

He slumps down on one knee, still clinging to the console, blood trickles down his chin …"she overloaded herself to defeat it."

He falls to the floor, dead …his new human body still on the printer table, unused. Archer tries to catch Biggs as he falls to the floor but he is also weak from the virus and lands kneeling next to him. He turns his eyes away from Biggs' limp mechanical body to look into Jennifer's eyes. She gets down next to Archer, supporting him from falling further. In the short time he has known Jennifer this way, it's the first time he has seen a helpless look from her as she breaks her gaze to see her processor crystal …herself, dimming. She returns her eyes to Archer's, no words are spoken as she cradles his weight to the ground. Archer is gone now too, she lies next to him with her head on his chest and her hand on his, for some time.

The blue glow of her processor, now completely extinguished …Jennifer convulses slightly as the connection is severed. Guinevere gets up and resumes the walk towards Ethan's empty suit. She acquires the fusion power kernel. Somberly, with a blank stare into nothing, she clicks it into place on her chest.

Chapter 12

Kylo opens his eyes …he takes a deep breath …he moves the transducing element away from his head. Lying still for a minute as memories compete in his head …distant memories of who he really is, slowly sweep back over his mind. Kylo knew Biggs better than anyone.

His true identity feels like a dream at first …but as he looks around the room he starts to remember what he knows to be true. He really is Kylo, not Biggs …he has been in a game. The dream feeling of Kylo and the realness of Biggs are actually reversed …he is Kylo. He notices the time, but he already knows he's been in the game for 47 minutes, because Biggs was 47 years old when he died.

Kylo sits up and looks over to see Zoey waking up on the table next to him, he figured it would be real soon because the virus infected them both at the same time. Zoey sits up, blinking his eyes, then gives his head a shake …digesting the experience in his mind.

"Hey my brother, how are you?" said Kylo.

Kylo and Zoey live in a reality where the speed of light is a little faster than the reality they experienced in the Earth game. The periodic table is a little different, but for the most part, the laws of physics are similar. In this world Kylo is 27 years old and Zoey is 28 in Earth game years …they are not gods, but ordinary beings just 75 years more advanced than those in the Earth game. The games are different here. While inside a game, it's the only reality they know. They go into a game intentionally to be any creature, but once inside one, they do not know they are in a game until their character dies. It is only then that they wake up, retaining the lifetime experiences of their character. It is a birth to death experience.

Still in a fog, Zoey turns to his brother, "I see why people can only handle a few games before they stop playing them. Kinda fills up your head, I feel more like Archer than who I am. Archer lived longer than I have been alive …it's weirder than I expected."

"Tell me about it," said Kylo …"what a crazy experience. I …I fell in love with Sheila, what's it going to be like seeing her now? I learned so much about life

…it's like living your life, learning from it, then getting a chance to live it again."

"Yeah man, I hear you …and I have never thought so much about our reality …but I will now."

"I did have a little trouble spawning into the game at first," said Kylo.

"Really? …what kind of trouble."

"Not really sure …the first try was unsuccessful, but then after a minute I got in just fine."

They both get up from their tables, they hug then kiss each other on the cheek. In their world it is a customary embrace after not seeing each other for a long time. Half of a lifetime certainly qualifies as a long time, but now, after the game, it feels super awkward to both of them.

"We …I mean the humans, they had a concept called Buddhism. I find it ironic that it's kind of what we did …when we went into and back out of the humanity game," said Kylo.

"Yeah that is bizarre," said Zoey …"but we made a U-turn and came back to this life. We were so curious about what would be outside our realm, while we were there all along. We were so curious about life after death, and when we died, we went back to where we were born."

"Brings new meaning to the term 'old soul'," said Kylo.

"No kidding …we spent all that time wondering if the universe came from something or nothing, turns out we came from us."

They both look up at the screen showing arrivals, departures, and room numbers.

"I noticed a glitch in the program," said Kylo …as he looks up Sheila's real name and Zoey looks up those important to him.

"What's that?"

"Some cats don't react at all when they see a mirror for the first time …I mean zip, nothing."

"I'm going to miss my Bear," said Zoey. They watch the screen update every few seconds. "The hard part is deciding on the ones you want to connect with when you come back."

"No doubt, it's hard," said Kylo …"some you clearly want to ..and should ….then there are the animals."

As they leave the room …"let's get some lunch," said Zoey, putting his hand on Kylo's shoulder …"and find your wife ..and our new friends."

Kylo looks over at Zoey …"yes ..and let's find our friends."

Zoey shows a hint of a smile …"we have a lifetime of memories to talk about." They walk away, down a ridiculously long hallway with lots of doors.

Chapters

Why is Archer quizzing Jennifer about the little robot?

Is the AI Jennifer a real person?

If Jennifer is real, do you think Zoey should connect with her or the original Jennifer?

What is Kylo talking about when he said he had trouble spawning into the game?

What did Kylo mean when he refers to the animals in the last chapter?

Define sentient, self-awareness and free will. Does free will exist? If so, does it exist at different levels in humans?

Why did Jennifer say perfection removes meaning from life?

Regarding hot water heaters, why would anyone want to heat hot water?

Can the really tough questions only be answered with logic and probability …without blind faith and without traditional science? …Why?

Do you believe that the abundance of whole number relationships in nature and the unreasonable usefulness of the periodic table, could be enough to say that we are created by a conscious mind? Combined with the digital nature of chemistry, does this indicate that we are in a simulation? Since a decision cannot be made without a reason, even for a godlike being, does this prove that we have a purpose? …even if we don't know what the purpose is?

In the simulation theory, why is it logical to believe that the program creator has at least some qualities in common with us?

If we are in a simulation, what is the irony regarding the possibility of eternal life?

Suggested Reading

The Hitchhikers Guide To The Galaxy,
by Douglas Adams, 1995

Free Will, by Sam Harris, 2012

Zero: The Biography of a Dangerous Idea,
by Charles Seife, 2000

The Inexplicable Universe: Unsolved Mysteries,
Audiobook, by Neil deGrasse Tyson

People to Follow

Elon Musk, Guardian of Humanity, SpaceX, Tesla
Zohreh Davoudi, Nuclear Physicist, MIT
Lisa Randall, Theoretical Physicist, Harvard
Max Tegmark, Cosmologist, MIT
David Chalmers, Philosopher, NYU

Notes

Notes

Notes

Notes